ALEX LIDELL

LAST CHANCE WITCH

IMMORTALS OF TALONSWOOD

TRIDENT RESCUE
Contemporary Romance
ENEMY ZONE
ENEMY CONTACT

POWER OF FIVE (7 books)
Reverse Harem Fantasy Romance

POWER OF FIVE (Audiobook available)
MISTAKE OF MAGIC (Audiobook available)
TRIAL OF THREE (Audiobook available)
LERA OF LUNOS (Audiobook available)
GREAT FALLS CADET (Audiobook available)
GREAT FALLS ROGUE
GREAT FALLS PROTECTOR

IMMORTALS OF TALONSWOOD (4 books)
Reverse Harem Paranormal Romance
LAST CHANCE ACADEMY (Audiobook available)
LAST CHANCE REFORM (Audiobook available)
LAST CHANCE WITCH
LAST CHANCE WORLD

Young Adult Fantasy Novels

TIDES

FIRST COMMAND (Audiobook available)

AIR AND ASH (Audiobook available)

WAR AND WIND (Audiobook available)

SEA AND SAND (Audiobook available)

SCOUT

TRACING SHADOWS (Audiobook available)

UNRAVELING DARKNESS (Audiobook available)

TILDOR

THE CADET OF TILDOR

SIGN UP FOR NEW RELEASE NOTIFICATIONS at https://
links.alexlidell.com/News

VICTOR

Standing at his office window in Talonswood Reform Academy, Victor surveyed the green, where cleaning crews dealt with the aftermath of the battle that had ended a few hours ago. That is to say, the battle that the witch Samantha Devinee had ended single-handedly by tapping into magic Victor had no idea she was capable of.

The ping of a computer behind him announced another video call starting up. It was the fifth such conference since the pack of fae savages had run rampant over the Academy green. To think, just a few centuries ago such a scrimmage wouldn't have risen to the level of dinner conversation, but now, with everyone being *civilized*, it was a worldwide outrage.

The council was oscillating between being livid over the attack and industriously planning what to do next—neither of which aligned with Victor's needs. His Talonswood Reform project was supposed to have been slow and simple: seed the acceptance of vampiric norms while molding the young witch into a loyal tool, guiding her toward the day when she had enough skill to seal the gateway portal to Talon. Finally, with

Samantha's help, he would rid the mortal world of fae once and for all, rendering the council obsolete. And creating a leadership void that Victor would happily fill.

Instead, he now had a grenade on his hands with the pin half-pulled. Or perhaps not.

Returning to his desk, Victor declined the incoming call and placed one of his own instead. In moments, his lead scientist Anton appeared on the screen, his pinched white face and starched lab coat foregrounding a gleaming modern research lab. The very best that Victor's money could buy.

"We need to speed up the timeline," Victor said, ignoring the pained look that flickered across Anton's features. With an immortal life span, patience was a vampiric virtue, but researchers took even that baseline to an exponential degree. *Speed up* was not in their vocabulary. "The witch's power has flashed quickly. Grooming her for several years is no longer an option, Anton."

Anton sighed, his thin silver brows knitting almost comically. "We've been over this, Your Excellence. Desire is required for the procedure to work. For the witch's magic to seal the gateway, she needs to *want* to seal it. That type of sentiment takes time to cultivate. It isn't just a matter of her magical strength."

"We don't all live in a laboratory, Anton," Victor snapped at the screen. "I intend to use compulsion to speed things along. Please skip the lecture on the dangers and tell me the status of CS3."

Compulsion Serum Third Generation—CS3—had been Anton's research focus for the past decade. He had to have something to show for all that time.

"It is still in clinical trials," said Anton.

"Indulge me," said Victor.

"CS3 enhances compulsion and adds amnesia. The subject

retains the desire to follow the suggested direction for several days without recalling the moment CS3 was first ingested," Anton said reluctantly. "The peak effect comes twenty-four hours after ingestion, unlike traditional compulsion that begins to fade immediately."

"In other words, if I compel the witch to close the gateway the day before I need it done, she will retain the desire to close it without remembering my discussing it with her." Victor nodded. That sounded promising.

Anton held up a hand in warning. "There are limitations, sir. Timing is everything. CS3 and the initial compulsion must be given when the target is agreeable with the goal." He waved his hand. "You must *first* have the witch naturally agree that closing the gateway is a good idea, *then* cement the desire with strong compulsion and clear direction. Finding a time when her mental defenses are exhausted and she feels antagonistic against the fae is key. The closure should be attempted at the twenty-four-hour mark postsuggestion."

"That isn't a great deal of time to plan an entry into the gateway building," said Victor.

"In a few years, you will have a better—"

"I understand." Victor cut Anton off. "What else?"

"CS3 is toxic. I cannot fully account for long-term effects, but it certainly can't be administered more than once—even if I had multiple doses. Which I do not."

"Then we will work with what we have," said Victor. "Have the dose delivered and switch your efforts to readying for the gateway closure. It appears we will be slaves to opportunity and will have only a short window to get things in place."

"Understood, sir." Anton hesitated. "Sir, everything I said, it is *experimental* and—"

Victor cut the line. He needed to get back to the circus the council was putting on. For now, they still had the power to destroy everything he'd worked for.

A computerized ping sounded again, and Victor opened the call, a pretty young brunette appearing on the screen. Sofia, the council's lackey. "Count Victor, do you have a situation report update for us?" she asked primly. Her wide blue eyes and smiling cotton-candy-pink lips were merely a well-designed front—the bitch was ruthless. "It would help if you turned the video on at your end, sir."

And she missed nothing.

"Of course," Victor said. Schooling his expression, he crossed his legs casually before turning on his camera. "The Academy grounds are fully secure from the fae attack. As for the genesis of the assault..." Victor tapped a finger on his desk, contemplating his answer. There was no way in hell Bryant had nothing to do with the attack, but however he'd done it, the fae king had covered all his bases. "Prior to succumbing to his injury, the one perpetrator we captured confessed to working for a group of humans calling themselves hunters. He and the others were paid to 'thin the herd' at Talonswood Reform while specifically extracting the witch. The hunters wished to question the witch personally and execute her at the pyre."

"Creatures working for human hunters. What is the world coming to?" Sofia made a *tsk* sound and shook her head, leaning toward the screen. The fae viper was going on the attack. "I'll be frank, Count Victor. The council has grave concerns about Academy security. You've assumed leadership of Talonswood Reform specifically to address security measures, yet the effect has been the opposite."

"I assure you—" Victor started.

"Don't kill the messenger, sir," Sofia interrupted, self-importance coating her words like perfume, "but I've been instructed to inform you that you have one month to get the Academy in order before the council initiates a series of stress trials, including surprise inspections and mock assault scenarios. Should Talonswood Reform fail, you will be stripped of your position. By custom, the next Academy dean would, of course, be fae."

"That sounds reasonable," said Victor, his cold blood chilling inside his veins. If he was terminated, he would be unable to so much as remain on the island without drawing suspicion, let alone continue his work with the witch. "Please inform the council that we welcome any measures they feel appropriate to test the Academy's defenses."

Clicking off the chat, Victor forced his clenched hands to open. Politician, master, strategist—he was all those things. What he *wasn't* was a bloody boot camp director.

Fortunately, there was someone under his command who was just that—and now that King Bryant's conflict with his bastard sons was established, there was no reason not to lean into Asher's expertise. The two of them might not be heading to the same destination, but for the time being, there was no better companion for Victor to travel with.

Leaning out of his office door, Victor called over the guard stationed there. "Get me Commander Asher," he ordered. "Now."

2

SAM

*S*am! Sam! Sam! A familiar voice purrs in my soul, the little green dragon that's taken residence in my dorm room flapping his wings. *His* wings. I'm certain that he's male, just as I'm certain that he's a dragon. That he's mine.

Or perhaps I'm his.

Still dressed in nothing but Reese's oversized shirt—my old clothes having been soaked in the bleach by Wayne and his gang several disasters ago—I rub one bare foot against my shin. Though the attack on Talonswood Reform ended a few hours ago, the scent of battle still clings to my skin. Standing beside me, Ellis and Reese—half of the once close-knit group of immortal friends who nicknamed themselves *horsemen*—smell of blood and sweat. Beyond the window, night settles gently over the wounded Academy, the green bathed in pale moon hues.

And here, inside my room…is a fire-breathing dragon. When my attention catches on him, the little creature coos and, opening a short green snout of tiny sharp teeth, melts my best pair of shoes into a bubbling leather goo. He burps a tiny puff of white smoke and turns to look at me, as if to make sure I saw it. His yellow eyes gleam with pride, the two stubby horns on his head shifting as his face splits in what can only be called a shit-eating grin. The spiky, spade-shaped tip of his tail swishes over the ground, casually toppling Mika's desk chair.

"Fuck," I mutter, the implications of what this might mean swiping at my thoughts. A dragon. I've never even had a dog, and now I'm somehow bonded to an overgrown lizard that flies and destroys furniture. In my side vision, I see the down feathers from my pillows now floating in the air, my wooden dresser shredded and smoldering at the edges. Fuck. Fuck. *Fuck.*

"What do I do with it?" I ask Ellis, who seems the most likely to know something about dragons. "Talk. In detail. And as quickly as you can."

Ellis runs a hand through his pale blond hair, his soft Scottish burr making mundane words sound musical. "When I first hired ye, it was to find a dragon egg. I didn't know that's what it was, only that there was something my father wanted that was hidden in a box and would open only for a witch. Things got a wee bit out of hand, you touched the egg, and it imprinted on you—like the duckling imprinting on rolling objects. My father has had it in Talon since. I didn't know it hatched, but apparently, it did and followed my father from Talon here to you. That's all I have."

"So is it like a familiar, then?" Mika says. Now that she has her laptop safely out of the dragon's reach, my tiny demifae roommate is back in her usual mode of trying to solve all problems online. The *tap tap tap* of computer keys as she speaks is comforting for its familiarity. "I thought that was just lore, but perhaps there's something to it. Though..." She frowns at her screen, impatiently flicking a strand of spiky black hair out of her eyes. Behind her huge teal glasses, her eyes narrow. "I think your familiar *should* be a cat."

"She isn't adopting from the pound, Mika," says Reese, pragmatically moving flammables out of the dragon's way. His black hair is tied back in a low messy bun, his thickly muscled bare torso painted with fae blood, dirt, and white streaks of dried sweat.

Mika ignores him and types more frantically—her typical reaction to stress. One of her feet, in a pink unicorn ankle sock, jiggles like a caffeine addict's. "Everything I'm finding points to cats. Not dragons. You can't have a dragon, Sam. That's just not...not done!"

"I'll name him Kitten," I tell her. "That's the best I can do. Now, does that dark web of yours say anything about what to do with him?"

"Cage him," says Reese, his voice low and dark, his ice-blue eyes flashing dangerously. "Preferably before Kitten burns down the building."

"You think I keep a cage in my room just for emergencies?" I wheel on Reese, my head starting to pound. In the past twenty-four hours I've been accosted by a pack of angry demifae who soaked me in bleach and locked me in the chem lab, trapped in the same chem lab with Reese while the building crumbled around our ears, walked out into a massacre on the green, summoned lightning, and now...now I'm fucking done with this day.

"There should be cages in the armory." Reese speaks directly to Ellis, as if I'm no longer an invited participant to the conversation. "We sometimes capture small game to train the demivamps needing to learn feeding and table manners."

I feel bile rise. All right. Maybe I'm glad Reese is addressing Ellis instead of me.

"Get one," Ellis says, his beautiful face determined and

calm. "I don't imagine we'll be able to keep Kitten a secret long, but it would be best if we disclose his existence on our terms and not via a barracks fire."

With a curt nod, Reese disappears from the room. Kitten waddles after him to the closed door and rakes his claws through the wood. When the door fails to open for him, the dragon twists around, scrunches up his face, and emits an ear-piercing shriek of discontent.

"Stop it," I snap at him.

The little stinker turns to me and spits a small stream of fire, stomping and flapping his spiny wings to add to the effect. I swear his iridescent green scales go teal and then purple for just a moment, as if a wave of anger slides physically just under his skin. Being the size of a very large cat, the temper tantrum is more dangerous than frightening, but problematic either way.

"Mika, please tell me you found something on training dragons that's not from Pixar or Disney."

The air around Ellis shimmers, his muscled body shifting into a snow-white wolf with intense golden eyes. Shaking his fur into its full predatory majesty, the wolf pulls his upper lip back into a snarl and advances on Kitten. My breath catches, each of Ellis's steps brimming with power and command so potent that I feel it echoing through the room.

Taking notice, the dragon turns toward the prowling predator and lets out another shriek that has Mika covering her sensitive vampire ears.

Not missing a beat, Ellis's wolf lowers his salivating muzzle to Kitten's level and emits a low guttural growl.

Kitten backs up toward me frantically, his sounds turning into frightened pitiful yelps as the little spikes on his snout seem to droop slightly. Big yellow eyes stare at me in desperation as the dragon backs right into my legs and wraps his tail around my left ankle.

"Easy," I tell Ellis's wolf, my chest tight. "You're scaring him."

"I'm pretty sure that's the point," says Mika.

Kitten whines pitifully again and trembles against my leg while the wolf's growl continues, dripping fangs on full display.

Before I can think better of it, I squat down and hold my arms out to the dragon, who hops happily into my hold, his small body vibrating with a purr that matches his name. Wrapping my arms around him, I pull the dragon to my chest, his small warm weight feeling perfect against me. Like a missing puzzle piece fitting into a hole I never knew existed.

The air around Ellis shimmers a second time, an irritated male taking the place of the previously irritated wolf. "What the bloody hell are ye doing, Devinee?" Ellis demands, looming over Kitten and me. The little puffs of smoke coming from the dragon's nose become faster at once. "That wee bugger can fry you to a crisp!"

"Well… You frightened him!"

"I bloody hope I did!" says Ellis. "Do you want him running amok and destroying everything?"

"Of course not." My arms close protectively around Kitten, whose scales are not at all cold like I thought a lizard's might be. "But you don't need to terrify him either. He just jumped into a new world, for fuck's sake. Do you know how stressful that probably is?"

"Yes, I imagine I have a damn bloody good idea."

Well yes, the male has a point. I bite my lip, the magic inside me undulating in swarms of buzzing bees. Kitten, meanwhile, apparently feeling braver from his place against my chest, lifts his head to stare triumphantly at Ellis's harsh features before breathing a thin stream of flame that catches the tip of the warrior's blond hair.

Ellis smothers the flame with his thumb and pointer finger and shifts his golden glare to me. His sharply carved jaw and cheekbones are rigid with barely checked frustration. "How do you propose to discipline him?" he demands.

"I don't know." Sighing, I look down at the dragon in my arms, his green scales shifting color slightly toward teal. "What am I gonna do with you?"

Kitten blinks back at me with large pleased eyes and…and sinks little razor-sharp teeth into my forearm.

Ellis's sword is out at once, the steel flashing. I twist my back to the male, shielding Kitten as the pain from the bite shifts into something strange and warm. Inside me, the buzzing bees of magic rushing chaotically through my blood now make a beeline for the dragon. A suckling sensation tickles my forearm, Kitten's contented purring filling the room as he drinks my magic in hungry little gulps.

3

ASHER

sher turned his face up to the cleansing rain. The copper scent of blood still hung thick in the air over the battle-ravaged green. Even in the dark of night, his fae vision picked up the devastation in excruciating detail—torn and pitted grass, dark pools of blood and tufts of fur, shattered lamps.

Snapping orders to the guards, he sent a second detail to reinforce the school perimeter, signed off on the head-count reports without slowing his stride, and requested a structural engineer to survey the damaged grounds the following morning. In the grand tapestry of warfare Asher had led, the evening skirmish was no more than a stumble.

But in the tapestry of peace between creatures, in everything that Asher had worked for in the last century, it was an unmitigated disaster. Not the rogue attack itself—the Academy was always a prime target, and Asher knew one assault or another was inevitable—but the response by fae and vamp factions at the school, both instructors and students…

Disgraceful, undisciplined chaos. Worse still, after failing to come together under fire, they weren't coming together to rebuild either.

With the arrival of Samantha and then Victor, the Talonswood Reform that Asher had built had been destroyed.

A wolfish whine caught his attention under the pattering rain, the sound filled with a soul-shattering mix of pain and terror. Changing his course, Asher jogged toward the huge pile of moss-covered stone and metal rubble that had been the science building's chemistry wing, the noise getting louder as he approached. His first thought was that a cadet had been caught in the collapse, pinned beneath a piece of the fallen wall. None of the cadets were supposed to be out in the science building at this late hour, but with Victor's gracious leniency, Asher could no longer predict what would and would not be permitted from day to day.

The pitiful whine came again, now overlapping with a pair of voices.

"Like the taste of your own filth, dog?" Christian, one of the demivamps and Victor's pet cadet, spat each venomous word one at a time, his French accent echoing from the stones.

A thumping that sounded like a boot landing against ribs sounded, followed by another howl of pain.

"An eye for an eye, Christian," Leanne, another of the demivamps intoned just as Asher leapt over the rubble. "That's only fair. It's our law."

Landing in a crouch, Asher spun around in time to see Leanne plunging a knife toward an injured first-year wolf cowering beneath one of the overturned lap tables. Lunging from his place, Asher wrapped his arms around the girl, tackling her to the ground as the knife sliced into his biceps.

A distant pain shot through him as he pushed himself off the enraged vamp and wrested the blade from her hand.

Behind them, Christian's fangs were extending, his normally cool, haughty features flashing with murderous hunger as he closed on the wolf. Light from one of the remaining wrought iron lamps glanced across his olive skin, giving it a ghostly pallor.

"Belay that!" Asher hollered, sweeping Christian's leg and sending the vamp tumbling backward. Scrambling up, Asher put his body between the wolf and vamps, his heart hammering against his ribs. "That's a cadet, Christian. A creature just like you. You can't feed on him."

"Like hell I can't!" Snarling, Christian rose into a crouch, his face bloody from where an arrow had taken his eye. The demi had enough vamp blood in him that the injury wasn't fatal—but the eye would not grow back. "The fucking wolves took my eye, and I want it back. Feeding on his blood will do it."

Asher moved with Christian, mirroring the boy's movements. "You aren't a full vampire. Even living blood won't bring back a limb."

"You don't know that," Christian snarled, the savage fury rolling off him saturating the air. "Fae blood may. Stop me from trying, and I'll rip out your throat."

Lunging forward, Asher grabbed the young vamp by the throat and slammed him into what was left of the nearby wall. Holding the boy off the ground enough that his toes barely skimmed the floor, Asher filled Christian's field of vision. Despite his vamp lineage, Christian's pulse beat savagely, his glazed expression only now showing a comprehension of who held him in check.

"Feed on a creature, and you will die," Asher snarled into the boy's face, making each word hard. Unquestionable. "That is our law."

"A fae-made law," the boy snarled back, but pulled in his fangs.

Throwing him to the ground, Asher waited until both demis stalked away from the rubble, their footsteps and shadows disappearing into the night. Then he lifted the injured wolf and started toward the infirmary in hopes that someone with more time and patience than himself could coax the cadet into shifting back.

Walking back outside onto a now-empty, mist-filled green some minutes later, Asher noticed a drawing on the previously clean infirmary wall. Stepping closer to examine the rendering, he marked a stick figure image of a pyre with a witch perched atop the flames. All drawn in blood.

Fucking hell. This was the new Talonswood Reform, forged in the twin flames of Victor's intrigues and Samantha's influence.

"Sir."

Turning toward the speaker, Asher found a guardsman with a message to report to the count's office. *Think of the devil.* Issuing orders to have the drawing cleaned, Asher took a calming breath and—reminding himself sternly that ripping Victor's throat out was not going to help—answered the summons.

"Commander Asher." Victor uncharacteristically rose when Asher entered, even going so far as to give him a respectful nod of the head. Even at this late hour, postbattle, the count looked as regal as ever in a black silk suit and crisply knotted blood-red tie, black hair swept away from his high pale forehead. His office was another thing entirely. Usually impeccably neat, it now had papers piled high on the desk, a couple of drawers pulled partway out. Coupled with a blinking printer light complaining about low ink levels, the room betrayed the amount of administrative headaches going on behind the scenes. Good. Victor *should* have headaches.

"Thank you for coming up," Victor continued, his Romanian accent slightly more pronounced than usual. "I have been going over the incident, and the more I examine it, the more I find myself realizing that if not for your leadership, our losses would have been a lot harsher."

"They're harsh enough, sir," Asher answered. "Nine cadets and one guardsman have succumbed to their injuries. At least three others are in critical condition. That's over double the butcher's bill such an attack should have inflicted had the Academy's defense posture been more appropriate."

"I see." Victor tilted his head, studying Asher carefully, black eyes seemingly bottomless in the low lamplight. Like a snake deciding just how far it would need to open its mouth to swallow a rabbit.

Except Asher was no rabbit. "I've requested a crew to fix the science building, which it appears the witch destroyed," he continued. "I'm unaware of what she was doing there to begin with, or how she obtained a key to a locked room." *But I have a fucking good guess.*

"She was there on my instruction," Victor said, crossing his legs as he settled back in his leather chair. "Practicing magic away from other students. A safety measure that seems all the more sensible now."

"Very good, sir." Asher's voice was stoic despite the last nail having just been driven into the proverbial coffin. Reaching inside his jacket, he withdrew the letter he'd penned an hour ago, when he'd returned to his quarters for a few minutes' respite. His chest tightened as he placed the paper on the polished wood of Victor's desk and gave it a small, excruciatingly difficult push. "My resignation."

Victor's eyes flashed for a moment before he got control of himself, picking the letter up with long pale fingers and looking it over carefully. Vamps liked to take their time—a trait that usually annoyed Asher, but not today. In fact, he appreciated the chance to quietly say goodbye.

Finally, Victor withdrew an expensive pen from the inside pocket of his jacket and scraped something on the bottom of the document before sliding the paper back.

It was done.

"Thank you, s—" Asher stopped midsentence. *Rejected.*

He blinked.

Neither the ink nor the serene expression on Victor's sharply angled face had changed.

"Is this a jest, sir?" Asher asked. Victor couldn't reject his resignation. The count was his superior here at Talonswood Reform, but he had no authority to keep Asher here against his will. More to the point, there was no reason for the vamp to want Asher here.

Victor tapped his desk, his nail making a *tick tick tick* sound against the polish. "I wish it were." Walking over to a shelf, he removed a decanter of whiskey and filled two crystal glasses, holding one out to Asher—a gesture signaling an equality in conversation, which the count rarely afforded a subordinate. "Not a joke, Commander. A request. Consider it an opening offer in a negotiation."

Asher shook his head, his fingers curling around the crystal. "With all due respect, sir, you've strived to undermine everything I stand for from the moment you arrived. My Academy was a place of ordered discipline that forged unity among creatures. Your version is a court with all its intrigues. You castrated the military discipline, introduced enough favoritism to encourage the fae and vampire cadets to start feuds, and even gave the witch leave to practice magic without my knowing it. Frankly, I've been nothing but a thorn in your side. Why in the name of anything that is logical would you want me to stay?"

"Because today's attack illustrated my shortcomings to me," Victor said simply. "Is it that difficult to believe that I can admit my mistakes?"

"Yes," said Asher.

Victor smiled, a faint upturn of his thin, red-tinged lips, and took a long sip of his drink. "All right, then. Let me lay my cards on the table, Commander. I believe in the vampiric court. I believe that vampires will and should rise. Both of those beliefs remain the same. However, I also falsely believed that the Academy was safe from the kind of attack we saw today. Perhaps more to the point, I will now be utterly consumed with the council's investigation. If you leave, there will be no one running the place."

Asher suppressed a snort. What Victor meant was that he was afraid he'd get kicked out of his position—which was likely to happen if the place didn't shape up to the council's standards.

"I think it's now obvious to us both that I am no military general," Victor continued, eyes crinkling warmly. "But you are. And the Academy needs a general right now. Tell me what your demands are."

"I have none. I'm done." Asher put down his glass. "I'm just fine with you getting kicked out, sir. And I'm not interested in executing your vision."

"You won't be," said Victor, capturing Asher's eyes with steellike intensity. "I am offering you full control of the students and none of the administrative headache. Anything with regards to their discipline and education, you have final say over. Not just now, but for the entire time you remain at Talonswood Reform. I will put that in blood for you."

Asher turned and started toward the door, his mind spinning, looking for the catch.

"And also"—Victor's low voice pinged against his back—"I'll give you the witch."

Asher paused.

"I got your attention there, didn't I, Commander?" The count's voice had turned just a bit singsongy.

Heat rose in Asher's veins, simmering his blood. He turned back toward Victor, summoning all his strength to keep his face impassive. "I don't believe the witch is yours to give."

"No, she is not. But this is where my stick comes in, Mr. Asher." Victor stepped in closer, all amusement and nonchalance now gone. "Samantha Devinee is more powerful than she knows. And more dangerous than she can imagine. Stay, and you have free rein to ensure she walks whatever straight and narrow you believe will ensure she doesn't crack the world open beneath our feet. Leave, and I will personally train her as I see fit."

"Is that a threat?" Asher felt a growl rise deep in his throat.

Victor cocked a dark brow. "It's a statement of reality. *Someone* needs to get the girl in check. If you don't, I will. My way."

Fuck. The bastard had a point. Asher breathed out a long slow breath. "Full control, Victor. You don't so much as order punishments, much less allow leniency for your pets. Nothing goes over my head. No double standard for vampires and fae and witches. No special considerations for vampiric protocol. I set all cadets' schedules and routines."

"Done," said Victor. "You can have all the runs and formations and fire watches you would like. But I do have one stipulation since we are speaking of equality. If my instincts are correct, neither Ellis nor Reese were able to keep their cocks to themselves when it came to Samantha Devinee. So here is my line in the sand, Asher: stick yours in the witch, and this whole Academy I'm about to give you on a silver platter, you lose it all. Show the witch any leniency, and I will ensure she gets double her due. I'll put *that* into our blood contract as well."

4

SAM

The shrill sound of an alarm jolts me from sleep, my sore muscles reluctantly pulling away from where I'm tucked against Ellis's hard body.

Across the room, Mika yelps. "What the hell is that?" Running barefoot to the window, she nearly trips over Kitten, who's snoozing on the floor. It figures that an alarm call loud enough to raise the dead fails to wake the little green monster.

"Morning formation." Out of bed in one smooth motion, Ellis pulls his pale hair back neatly, neither the noise nor its meaning fazing him one bit. I have to drag my eyes away from his bare torso and chest, his ridged muscles creating shadows in the gray predawn light, black joggers just clinging to the crests of his hips. "It looks like Asher is back in charge."

"This used to be a daily occurrence." I rub the heels of my hands against my eyes. Unlike Ellis, who seems trained to go from deep slumber to battle ready in 1.5 seconds, I'm still getting my bearings. Including the fact that beyond my dorm window, the sun is just now beginning to rise. Between settling down Kitten and getting the room into some semblance of order, I've barely gotten four hours sleep. Asher's timing is impeccable, as always.

"Get dressed," Ellis orders with a tight jaw. "Both of you."

"What are we going to do with Kitten?" I rummage through the drawer in search of something the dragon didn't destroy last night. My PT kits didn't make it. "And you think Asher would rather I show up to formation naked or wearing this?" I hold up the charred remains of a blue shirt.

"I'll get you one of mine," Ellis says. "As for the wee beastie…" He pulls open the cage Reese fetched last night, and I frown at the uninviting metal. In the hallway outside our door, cadets' voices are already echoing off the walls, the demifaes especially fearing to be late.

"Alternatively, you could just take him with you. I've no doubt that the best way to break the news to Asher is to show up with a pet dragon in tow," Ellis says, still holding open the cage door.

Right. Sliding my hands under the warm green reptile, I hold my breath as I lift him, his paper-thin iridescent wings drooping lazily over my arms. At about fifteen pounds, he's heavier than he looks. Placing him gently in the cage and closing the latch with a soft click, I let out a breath. Besides puffing a bit of smoke from his nostrils, the dragon stayed asleep through the process—which is a whole lot more luck than I have any right to expect.

By the time we step out onto the green, the other cadets are already in formation, heavy mist swirling around their damp boots. The sun hasn't broken over the buildings yet, but birdsong rings from the densely crowned trees. The grass is patchy and scarred by battle, but—thankfully—body-free. Just another reminder of how cruel Asher's timing is, only hours after these cadets fought for their lives on this very ground.

Their sleep-befuddled faces reflect my own state of mind

as Asher strides sternly up and down their ranks, intimidating in black fatigues that cling to his every muscle. His sharp golden-brown eyes narrow on Ellis, Mika, and me as we file into the back, the flash of displeasure in them enough to make blood chill—usually. This morning, I truly have bigger worries than whether Asher is happy with the second hand on his stopwatch.

Standing behind Asher, Reese gives me a worried glance, and I summon a hint of a smile for the warrior. We survived the night. For the moment, that needs to count as victory.

"It has been a long twenty-four hours," Asher says, pitching his voice to carry across the green. "For some of you, possibly the longest twenty-four hours of your lives. And your day is not going to get any shorter."

Oh, you have no idea. I glance at Ellis, who gives me a hard shake of his head in warning and returns to attention like a perfect soldier.

"In the age of sail, the man-o'-war I served on beat to quarters every day," Asher continues. "All ships did. This means the ship cleared everything and prepared for battle as a matter of daily routine. Get used to it. Because today begins a new age at Talonswood Reform, one where vigilance is going to be your reali—"

Sam? Sam! Sam! The familiar voice inside my soul calls in a mix of confusion and irritation. *Sam! Sam! Sam!*

Shit. I shift my weight, glancing at Ellis. "Kitten's awake," I murmur to him under my breath.

Ellis keeps his gaze straight ahead. "Understood."

"'Understood' doesn't help very much," I hiss.

"Samantha." Asher's voice booms across the green, all eyes shifting to me. Striding toward me, the large male plants himself less than a foot away, his broad shoulders blocking out the rising sun. In the morning light, his golden hair looks like flame, his perfectly chiseled face and tawny eyes flashing with anger and warning. "Is there some other place you need to be right now?"

"Well, now that you mention it, sir—" I cut off as Ellis shakes his head. Asher misses nothing, shifting his weight to somehow make himself more menacing. He towers over me, every muscle in his broad chest outlined by his tight wicking T-shirt. A chill wind blows into my face, bringing with it his earthy sandalwood scent mixed with a heavy dose of reality. The tall male standing in front of me is the one who keeps discipline in the school—and it's of the bloody variety.

"Is there a problem, Commander?" Victor strides across the green toward us, the sunrise giving his face a faint red glow. In his tailored business suit and gleaming black shoes, he looks just as out of place amidst our combat boots as usual—and no less intimidating. Several of the demivamps, including Christian, drop to their knees as Victor walks by, but instead of taking the respect as his due, the count snaps his slender fingers and motions the cadets to their feet. "Not on Commander Asher's time, Christian," he drawls, "as you've no doubt noticed there has been a change."

A second wave of unease rolls through the courtyard as Victor stops slightly behind Asher, neatly underscoring his words.

"Nothing that an extra three miles for all first years this morning won't address," Asher says, his gaze never leaving me. "No one is to secure from the run until every last cadet is on the finish line. Don't keep your year mates waiting too long, Devinee."

"Yes, sir." I try to sound appropriately contrite, I truly do, but Kitten's insistent calling inside me dwarfs the problems in the courtyard. My gaze flickers to Reese in hopes of help, but the male only raises his palms slightly. Nothing he can do.

Then again, he doesn't know I have a dragon screeching inside my mind right now.

"Good. Then get going." Asher orders. The ranks of cadets before us immediately start toward the jogging trails while Asher crosses his arms to watch the procession. "Christian, lead them out on a five-mile loop."

The demivamp sprints to the front, the patch over his eye midnight black against the sunrise. Drawing a deep breath, I fall in line behind Mika. I wish the magic that managed to call up lightning could do something about my legs feeling like lead, but if anything, each step feels more difficult than the last.

Sam! Sam! Sam! Inside me, Kitten's voice changes from irritation to panic, and the edge of the green suddenly feels miles away.

My heart quickens, pain starting inside my body, feeling like a bungie cord that stretches farther the more distance I try to put between myself and the dorm. "Ellis." I grab his arm, my fingers digging into his hard muscle. The male grabs my elbow, catching me before I manage to fall onto my face. "Something is wrong."

"Agreed." Jogging beside me, Asher looks down at me from his towering height, his jaw hard as steel. "Wherever you seem to have left your mind today, Devinee—"

That is as far as he gets before the dorm room window shatters behind us and Kitten makes a dive for Asher.

5

SAM

I jump in front of Asher, taking the brunt of Kitten's impact against my chest as I fall onto my ass. On the other end of the green, the cadets who have not yet disappeared into the wooded trail now turn to stare, the whole of the Academy seeming to take a single collective breath—before dissolving into chaos.

Within moments, several of the fae cadets have shifted into wolf form, their muzzles pulled back to show salivating fangs. The vamps clump together, the strongest taking point while the weaker ones work to collect their pack mates together.

I watch their faces as they see Kitten curl into me protectively, as they process that the great ferocious dragon they've gathered together to slay is about the size of a very large winged cat, and breathe out a sigh of relief as the battle-ready posture turns to fierce whispers. I can't exactly blame them. From what I remember of history, dragons are to Talon what dinosaurs are to the normal world. Extinct. Or supposed to be.

Stepping away from where Kitten and I scramble to our

feet, Asher looks impressively unfazed, as if impossible creatures fly into his sphere of existence all the time. "Explain."

"We think this is her familiar," Ellis offers, his hands going into his pockets. "The hatchling from that egg Father tried to obtain. The little guy seems to have hatched from *the egg* and followed Bryant from Talon, and now we have this happy reunion." Ellis's emphasis on the word "egg" makes Asher's face lift slightly in sudden comprehension. Apparently, the male knows about the original heist that landed me here.

Burrowing into my chest, Kitten turns himself around to face Asher and snap his sharp little teeth at the male. His spade-shaped tail curls around the back of my neck, resting possessively against my collarbone.

"I tried to leave him in a cage," I offer by way of an olive branch, though I'm not sure there's anything anyone can say that would actually appease Asher. "But it seems he might have broken out of that. Or maybe he melted it. I'm not quite sure what happened."

Moving with deliberate slowness, Asher places his hands behind his back and surveys the green. "Christian," he bellows, "continue the run. I am holding you personally responsible for ensuring that every cadet except Devinee and Ellis start and finish the loop." After getting the cadet's acknowledgment, Asher turns back to Ellis and me. You two— you *three*—follow me."

Leading us behind the administrative building, Asher silently sets a course down a trail I've never seen before, pale early sunlight filtering through dense green pines. It's silent but for the trilling birds, Asher's stiff, broad back giving nothing away. About a mile into the hike, the wooded path gives way to rocky outcrops, tall granite buttresses jutting out of the hillside. Riding on my shoulder, Kitten curls his talons around my flesh, the sharp nails chafing me through the shirt. My worry about him falling quickly dissipates to an acknowledgment that, unlike me, Kitten has wings and that my tripping over my own feet under the extra weight is the greater concern.

As if to punctuate that thought, my boot catches a root, sending me sprawling on the ground while Kitten takes flight, squeaking indignantly.

"You all right?" Ellis extends his hand as Asher turns back toward the commotion.

I climb to my feet and tip my face toward the sky, where the tiny green dragon is now circling like a hawk, morning sun glowing through his wings. "What if he doesn't come back?"

"I don't imagine us to be so lucky," says Asher. "However, I believe this is far enough."

This, I realize, taking a good look at my surroundings, is a rock-filled plateau at the base of the larger slopes. Both beautiful in its starkness—and empty of most things that could catch fire.

Ah. Point for Asher.

"I hadn't thought of finding a place like this," I say.

"There are a lot of things you haven't thought of, Devinee." Putting his hands behind his back, Asher regards me for a long moment, his cold scrutiny making a shiver run down my spine. "You and Ellis both."

Ellis cocks a brow.

"This cannot continue," Asher says after the silence stretches long enough to have me shifting my weight from foot to foot. "The lack of discipline, the extracurricular activities, the parallel world that Samantha seems to create around herself. Talonswood Reform is returning to its roots. That means we have cadets here, not fae and vampires and witches and seasoned warriors playing games. Creatures got hurt. Cadets got hurt. The damage the Academy has sustained in the past two months has not been seen since its creation centuries ago. No more."

Ellis leans against a rock and snorts softly. Next to his militant, straight-backed half brother, Ellis's sinewy, latent muscle and wrinkled training gear give him the vibe of a drowsy panther. "You've made some kind of deal with Victor, haven't you? The Academy is yours again?"

Asher nods. "Yes. And in return, I will deliver to the council an Academy that does what the hell it's supposed to be doing: getting cadets ready for a time when they can integrate with the humans without drawing attention to themselves and exposing us all."

"I take it my dragon is a thorn in your reintegration plan?" I say, receiving a cold look.

"You are the thorn," says Asher, tawny eyes holding me in place. "The dragon is incidental."

Ellis crosses his arms over his broad chest, the sleeves of his blue PT uniform cutting into his biceps. "Why did you bring us out here, Asher?" he asks quietly.

"To tell you that this charade you are playing is over. You are not a cadet here, Ellis, and whatever game Bryant wanted to play with you watching Samantha, that skit has run its course. Pack. Don't pack. I don't give a damn as long as you are off the grounds before lunch."

My chest tightens, and it's all I can do to keep from reaching out to grab Ellis's arm as I wait for the warrior to respond. Asher can't be serious. Ellis can't let him be. Not now.

"Asher." Ellis's voice is softer than I'm used to, and that in itself spurs my anxiety. "Please."

"No." Turning on his heels, Asher takes a step toward me, glaring down from his daunting height. "As for you, Samantha, the special treatment you've enjoyed thus far is done. Studying magic on your own is done. Going off campus is done. I want to know where you are at all times. Trust me when I tell you that you do not want to discover what happens if you take one step without my knowing about it."

Cassis. The bar. Ellis. My throat closes, and, as if summoned by my distress, Kitten dives down into my arms. I press him against my chest on instinct, the little dragon hissing at Asher the way I wish I had the guts to. "What about him?" I ask.

"You will be reassigned quarters to a chamber that will not burn. The dragon will remain there until such a time as you can control him to ensure safe behavior." Asher nods to no one in particular before stepping away. "That is all. Dismissed."

Before I can open my mouth to protest, the air around Asher shimmers, a gold-streaked white wolf taking his place and trotting off.

THE NEW ROOM Asher promised turns out to be an upper level of the dungeon. The floor is covered in dark, rusty stains that can only be one thing, and the fourth wall is made of iron bars. A tiny barred window near the ceiling provides tendrils of sunlight that run in parallel patterns across the cold stone. Setting a newly acquired stack of uniforms into a metal trunk someone dragged in here, together with a metal bunk and fire-retardant blankets, Mika tries for a smile.

"At least it's a lot bigger than our place. And it's not like you don't have a key to the door. Think of it like living in a castle." She jerks her chin toward Kitten, who's making leisurely circles beneath the tall ceiling. "And he can fly here."

I press my shoulders against the stone, the walls seeming to close in on me despite the ample space. "He can also fly outside."

"Devinee." The sound of Ellis's voice has me straightening. Looking toward the exit, I find the male with his hand not quite touching the iron. "I'd knock, but iron and I don't get along too well."

Mika opens the door for him and slips out before I can say a word.

Seeing Ellis in a pair of washed-out jeans and a gray V-neck that clings to his pecs, I feel my heart sink farther into my belly. The male should be wearing a uniform. But maybe I'm wrong. Maybe they've come to some other arrangement. "Did you talk to Asher?" I ask hopefully, coming up to meet him halfway. His clean male scent wraps around me, calming my frantic nerves.

"Aye." Ellis slides a rough finger across my cheekbone, hooking it under my chin to raise my face up to meet his golden eyes. "Asher is set on his orders. This Academy, its mission—it's what he's spent a better part of a century building up. He believes in what he's doing, and he's not going to change that."

"We aren't stopping him from doing anything." The words slip out rougher and more desperate than I expect. After everything that we went through, after Ellis's refusal to go to Talon with his father, I don't understand how he can step away from the Academy with no more than a casual chat with his brother. I grab his wrist, the magic inside me flaring at the contact and sending a zing of energy that I'm certain the male feels too. "How is your being here hurting anything?" I demand. "And if Asher is so keen on saving lives, maybe he should look at some security footage. Something about you and your sword cutting down the attackers while everyone ran around like chickens with their heads cut off."

"Asher can't have me here because he knows I will protect you," Ellis says, his smoothly sculpted face and golden eyes tight with something I can't read. "And he isn't wrong."

"What the fuck is wrong with you protecting me?"

"The same thing that was wrong with Victor protecting the demivamps." Ellis's grip on my chin tightens with his words, gaining an edge of steel. "I don't like it any more than you do, Devinee, but it is a done deal. I will be in the main town, and I will see you when you earn the privilege of leaving these walls."

"That could be a fucking week or a year, Ellis! And you know it." I try to pull away, but he doesn't let go.

"Aye. And I'm immortal. I can wait out either one. Until then, you need to mind Asher. And keep your distance from Reese as well. I'm certain Asher will read Reese the riot act, but don't tempt the situation."

I shove Ellis's chest, which only has the effect of nearly knocking myself backward. "That's it? You don't want to fight this? You want to roll over like a pup and let—" I cut off as a growl echoes from Ellis's chest, his body vibrating with a growing anger that mirrors my own. This time when I try to shove him away from me, the male traps both of my wrists in one large hand and leans his face so close to mine that I can see his long blond eyelashes.

"What I want, Samantha, is to grab you by the scruff of the neck and drag you off somewhere where I can protect you for the rest of your life. But given that you have other hopes for the future than being my damn pet, you're going to have to learn to survive by the rules of this world. And Asher is right, I can't step aside and bloody watch it happen." He leans closer still, his scent filling my nose and making my sex clench as he scrapes his canines along my neck. "But I do think I better leave you with a reminder of what kind of power you're dealing with here."

Before I can respond, before I can so much as draw a breath, Ellis steps into me until my back is against the cold stone wall, the hard, pulsing bulge in the front his jeans digging into my hip.

6

ELLIS

*E*llis pressed Sam against the stone wall, inhaling her sweet and citrusy scent with predatory need. Beneath his grip, her heart hammered against her chest, her body pulsating with life and need and magic that made his head spin. *His. She was his.* The overwhelming possessive instinct drove through him with every beat of his own heart, the need to claim her washing over his self-control. Ellis's breath quickened, his body tightening with the urge to take his mate hard enough to mark her as his. Shit.

He'd wanted Sam before. Had taken her before. But not like he wanted to take her now.

Gripping each of her wrists in his hands, Ellis raised them above her head and loomed over her, his face inches from hers. Her red-streaked hair flowed around her high cheekbones like fire, highlighting the pink in her soft, full lips. Her hazel eyes sparked with a shadow of the same hunger that clawed at his insides, the scent of her arousal drifting from beneath that plaid uniform skirt, where the panties were no doubt moist with need.

But a mortal need that had no true notion of what he wanted. Of the mating frenzy his blood called for. "I want to take you, Samantha," Ellis rasped, his control on his body so tenuous that he braced his weight on the balls of his feet, ready to bolt for the door if she said no. "Hard. Very hard."

Sam's hazel eyes flashed their defiance, and, leaning forward, she sank her teeth right into the base of his neck. The sudden sting released a storm inside him that would stay at bay not a moment longer.

Reaching beneath Sam's skirt, Ellis tore off her panties in a decisive motion, the soaked cotton slick in his hand. Sam's eyes widened for a single moment before he grabbed her hips and twisted her around to face the wall, her hands bracing on the stone. Kicking the girl's thighs apart, he stroked her hot folds, not bothering to be gentle as he found her opening and thrust a finger inside her tight channel.

Sam let out a gasping moan, rising onto her toes from the intrusion even as her body clamped greedily around it. Her backside jutted out for more contact, which Ellis was more than ready to offer.

Pumping his finger in and out, he kicked her legs farther from the wall, taking the witch's balance as he added a second finger to her opening. A third.

Sam danced on her toes, her body writhing along his hand, looking for a purchase that she could not get. Freeing himself from his zipper, Ellis gripped Sam's hips and lifted her onto him, his cock sheathing itself inside her with a single brutal thrust that had her screaming against the walls of the stone chamber. For a moment, the more rational part of Ellis wondered whether the dragon might not descend upon them both with claws and flame, but even that thought couldn't stick. He didn't care about anything but the *thrust thrust thrust* of his shaft into his mate's hot, tight body, each pump sending a cascade of sensation from his cock to his spine.

Sam's toned body was strong yet vulnerable beneath his hands, her feet lifting off the ground with each stroke. Her fingers clawed the stone, the scent of her arousal mixing with the citrusy tang that filled Ellis's lungs with each breath. If he reached down to taste her moisture, he was certain he would feel lemongrass along his tongue. It was her scent. The scent of his mate. Reaching around, Ellis found the swollen hood around Sam's clit and stroked over it with the tip of a finger callused from centuries of weapons training.

Her breathing hitched, her barely contained moans of need rising to desperation as her luscious hips moved wildly in search of more contact. He pulled his hand away from her clit, and she growled, driving herself harder onto him. When he stroked the hood again without warning, he nearly came at the keening sound that escaped the little witch's mouth. He bent his face, using his teeth to pull aside the top of her blouse and reveal the glistening skin of her smooth shoulder.

Ellis ran his tongue along the smooth saltiness, savoring the taste and the thin tremor running over the witch's tight body. The blazing need was an urgent mass along his spine, his cock pulsing so hard that each beat of his heart made his head swim. Forcing himself to hold out despite his body's screaming protest, Ellis wrapped one hand tightly around Sam's waist, the other right atop the pulsing tip of her engorged clit. With the next thrust, he grazed that bud and sank his teeth and cock as far into her as they would go.

Sam screamed, her shuddering release echoing through the stone. Her whole body constricted around him, her muscles tightening in waves that sent blazing heat searing through his cock, his sac. Ellis' own body tightened, everything narrowing down to a single point so potent that pleasure and pain blended together. He shouted from the pressure as he made himself endure the need, waiting until Sam's spasms just began to subside before he ran his fingers over that clit one more time, making the witch come again as he released himself deep inside her.

7

———

SAM

*E*llis shifts me in his arms, settling down on the floor. I sit sideways in his lap, my cheek pressed against his bare collarbone. The denim of his jeans feels strangely rough beneath my backside, his fresh forest scent cocooning me as much as the contours of his rock-hard body. I feel woozy, the intensity of the pleasure still sending tiny tingles along my skin. My sex aches with a deep pleasurable heat that makes my cheeks warm in memory of what just happened. Of how much I enjoyed the primal savagery of it even as it drove me to my toes. Reaching up to the stinging along my neck, right at the base of my shoulder, I feel something slick and warm beneath my hands. My fingers pull away red with blood.

Ellis gently tilts my head to the side, his tongue lapping the wound as he cradles me against him. The safety of his touch should feel strange after what we just did, but it doesn't. It feels…natural.

"Samantha," he whispers, moving a strand of hair away from my face, his perfect lips hovering above my own. His white-blond hair is loose around his face—wild, like the wolf he is. His golden eyes meet mine with an intensity that makes my sluggish breath quicken, my magic waking in a songlike tremor inside my blood. "You are mine, Samantha. Body and soul and blood. My mate. I know you don't fully understand what that means now, but…I love you. More than love you. That's as well as I can explain."

He swallows, his face stilling with a heart-wrenching vulnerability. This strong male, who can face down a pack of vicious wolves without flinching, now looks at me with a desperation that twists my soul. I lift my hand, and Ellis holds still as I brush my thumb along his sharp cheekbone and the hard angle of his jaw. On the side of his neck, his pulse beats a powerful, too-fast tempo, his chest still.

"I love you too," I whisper, brushing my lips over his with a gentleness that contrasts the taking as much as fire and ice. As much as a witch and fae.

Ellis returns my kiss, his mouth slow and deliberate as he takes mine in, tasting and exploring as if it were the first time our lips connected. And in a way, it is. Pressing deeper into him, I put my hands on the male's shoulder and nudge him down to the ground until his broad back is flat on the stone and I'm straddling his hips. Reaching behind me, I find his erection growing in response to my hand, his quick intake of breath against my mouth confirming the arousal I feel.

With a final suckle along Ellis's tongue, I sit up and ease myself onto his erection, my aching channel chafing as the great width of him slides deep inside me.

"Sam," Ellis warns, his beautiful face filled with concern. "Are you sure you're—"

I silence him with a finger to his lips and run my hands along his washboard abdomen, each ridge hard as stone beneath my fingertips. Hard as the cock pulsing with increasing desperation inside me. Bracing myself on Ellis's hips, I slide up and down his shaft, slow and steady, feeling each moment of the connection with a sweetness that's made only more wonderous by the desperate hitch of the male's breath.

"You bit me," I inform him.

Ellis swallows, his fingers white where they try to grip the stone floor. Beneath me, his hips are already rising and falling, trying to coax me into a faster rhythm. I dig my nails into his pecs and resist his efforts, drawing a sharp breath out of him. "Aye," Ellis says, his low voice just a bit higher than normal. "Aye, I did. I marked you."

I lift his shirt, my hand circling his pectorals. "And how shall I mark you in return?" I muse, my eyes widening the moment the words spill from my mouth.

Sienna.

Shit. Shit. Shit. "I—"

Ellis's hands close over my cheeks, his body stilling as his gaze holds mine. "It's all right," he says, shaking his head at the expression of horror that I know grips my face. "I want you to mark me, Samantha. In any way you choose. That's the difference, aye? I want to give myself to you just as I want to take you as mine."

Relief floods my body, and Ellis's eyes twinkle. "Not that you could. You are only on top because I let you be."

Before I can respond to that challenge, Ellis rolls us over, his cock still inside me as he holds himself over my body. When I open my mouth to protest, he seals his own over mine, his laugh low and masculine as he picks up the thrusting right where I left off.

Ellis goes slow this time, taking command of my body with excruciatingly patient motions as all my nerves rekindle, buds of excitement unfurling through my body. My channel tightens around the male's cock in a demand for *more more.*

Breaking off the kiss, Ellis sits back and grabs the backs of my knees, positioning my legs on either side of his broad shoulders. Suddenly, there is nothing gentle about the thrust of his cock, the vulnerability of having my ass off the ground stupidly adding to the excitement. A knowing grin passes over Ellis's face, as if he knows exactly what the exposure is doing to me. Because, fuck it, the bastard does. He and Reese made sure of that.

Ellis grips my thighs and drives his cock into me so hard the *slap slap slap* of his sac against my slick skin echoes through the room. Need builds to pressure inside my core, my fingers digging into the floor and finding no relief. The abyss of another orgasm opens before me, so very close. And yet the hair's-width distance from it is insurmountable. My toes curl, my fingers clamping into fists. The thick head of Ellis's cock fills me completely, striking just the right spot deep inside me, over and over and over.

The last of my self-control fails me as I buck against him with all my strength, all my *magic*, the force of it shoving out like a pressure wave that strikes Ellis right in the chest. The male jerks, his eyes widening in surprise.

Without missing a beat, he pulls out of me and lands a stinging slap right into the center of my ass. The magic regresses right back in instinctual contrition, the loss of Ellis's cock inside me as punishing as the blazing fire he just erupted along my ass cheeks. I whimper once.

Nodding with approval that sends more pleasure through me than it should, Ellis grips my thighs again, but this time, this time he brings my sex to his mouth and sucks right on my clit.

I don't whimper as the orgasm rushes through me—I scream. And then scream again as he replaces his cock, thrusting twice before pouring his own release deep into me with a shout that echoes off the stone walls.

～

"So...that was new," I say a few minutes later as we both regain our breath. Ellis has rolled onto his back and settled me like a rag doll across his muscled body. "I don't even know how the magic escaped, much less in that form."

His grunt is laced with a mix of thought and amusement. "But I know exactly how to make you put a leash on it," he says into my ear.

My ass and face burn at once, and Ellis's rumbling chuckle vibrates beneath me. "Stop thinking like some human once told you you should." Wrapping his arms around me, he rolls into a sitting position, settling me beside him as his face turns serious. "That said, the coupling does appear to unlock more of your power, doesn't it?"

I rub my face, reluctantly returning to reality as Kitten chooses this moment to land between us and prod Ellis with his snout. "Thank you for not roasting us in the middle of, err, recreation," I tell the dragon, wincing as I consider the disaster that could have been.

Ellis scratches Kitten's chin. "I think we've an enthusiastic voyeur here, actually." He tips his head to regard the creature. "Or is it the magic that you enjoy, wee beastie? Was there more leaking out than that shock wave I felt?"

Kitten purrs in contentment and curls into a ball, tucking his head under his wing. I can't be certain, but I think he's as drained as I am. And as satisfied. "I hope Mika finds something more substantive on familiars than getting me a bootleg copy of *How to Train Your Dragon*."

Ellis snorts and rises smoothly to his feet, buttoning his

jeans and tying back his hair with quick movements until he looks as fresh and put-together as when he first walked in. Which reminds me…

"So what now?" I ask, straightening my own clothes. "Asher gets to flex his authority like a child with a new toy, and there's nothing to be done about it?"

Ellis rocks back on his heels, his hands in his pockets as he looks down at me from that perfect lethal body of his. At first I think that the flatline set of his mouth is a scowling agreement, but then a bit of amused breath escapes as the male gives up the façade and shakes his head.

"What's so funny?"

"I sometimes forget just how new you are to all this, but then something like your description of Asher brings it back." Amusement fades from Ellis's face as he steps up to me, his forest-fresh scent washing over me. "Asher is no child, Devinee. He is one the greatest military minds I've met—and the only creature in this world in whose care I would leave you. He will do well by you, Sam, if you let him. And if you don't…" Ellis presses his fingers against the angle of my jaw, his touch powerful and hard as steel. "He will *still* do well by you. Whether you think it so at the time or not."

8

SAM

I wake alone, the rehabilitated stone chamber feeling like a tomb despite its size. I'm cold and my body aches from sleeping on a hard cot, the fire-retardant blanket providing little by way of actual heat. Though maybe there is no amount of heat that would make this converted dungeon into something that doesn't resemble a prison cell.

Swooping down to me, Kitten hits me in the chest, his nose burrowing toward my arm. My magic awakens at the dragon's demanding nuzzle, and I brace myself as tiny little prickles sink into my skin, the strange sensation of Kitten's sipping not altogether unpleasant. But it is draining. Fortunately, coupling with Ellis yesterday seems to have refilled my magic reserves— an unexpected benefit of the mind-blowing orgasms. I hope my magic works out a way to refill itself without the help of a male's cock, though.

Thinking of Ellis makes me remember the instinctual way I pushed him with magic, something I would never have been able to do before—by instinct or not. "Is that what you're doing, little guy?" I ask Kitten. "Are you changing my magic, or at least my control of it?"

Kitten shifts constantly in my arms. The size of a very, very large winged cat, he straddles the line between lap animals and something way too big to carry around. And yet I already can't imagine how I ever lived my life without him.

Holding his body tightly against mine, I press my face against his warm scaly skin. For someone who is so used to being without other people, the isolation away from Mika and Ellis and Cassis shouldn't hurt nearly as much as it does.

Maybe I've gone soft, relying on Ellis, on Mika, on Cassis. On a network of friends who could be taken from me at a drop of a hat. Or, in the current case, a tyrant's rise to power. I brush my hand down Kitten's scales as a new burst of panic rushes through me. Can Asher somehow take Kitten away from me as well? After all, I never imagined he'd take away Ellis, but I was wrong there, wasn't I?

Separating Kitten's mouth from my arm, I look the dragon in the eye. "No more burning things down, you understand?" I say. "Or Asher will make me lock you in the dungeon room."

Kitten blinks his big yellow eyes innocently, the long black pupils pulsing wider and narrowing again.

Reaching inside me to where I can feel my bond with Kitten curled up in my soul, I draw a mind image with the magic. Fire. Kitten. The door to our dungeon cell slamming shut. "Do you understand?" I ask without much hope.

To my surprise, the magic shifts, forming an answering image. Asher running with his ass on fire.

"Yeah. No. Absolutely not." I focus on the sight of the locked door again and eventually feel a reluctant consent flow through the bond. Who knew communicating with Kitten would be like magical Pictionary?

~

THE BLARING alarm calling everyone to morning formation sounds muted through the dungeon's stony walls. Through the tiny window near the ceiling, I can see faint sunlight glancing through tufts of grass, but no sky. Opening the metal trunk, I pull out my PT uniform and stare helplessly at Kitten. Asher was clear about wanting the dragon kept isolated until he is trained, but Kitten has needs. Bodily ones as well as social ones. Right.

Reaching back into my magic, I imagine the sky, the strands of magic drawing Kitten's silhouette against the clouds. "Can you do that?"

The image inside my magic tickles as Kitten shifts it. Right back to Asher running with his ass on fire.

I glare.

Kitten puffs a bit of smoke at me, which I take for about as much agreement as I can hope for.

Letting him out of our cage, I feel a moment of gratitude as the dragon soars to the sky before I trudge out to find out what our lord and master has planned for fun on this fine day.

The plan, unsurprisingly, starts with Asher reading us the riot act while Victor nods along in full agreement. Apparently, we are all a sad lot of undisciplined juvenile delinquents who are a disgrace to earthworms. And since we need things spelled with as few letters as possible, the common infractions and consequences have now been posted in all academic buildings and barracks, the way they used to hang Articles of War on age-of-sail warships. Of special interest, Asher points out, is an hour of cleaning up the Academy grounds for every minute anyone is late for anything and six lashes apiece for anyone caught fighting or leaving campus. And the cherry on top of the shit sundae, if someone secures from a task before every single goddamned creature is finished and accounted for, everyone starts that task over from the beginning.

In other words, Ellis's great-minded brother Asher has gotten nostalgic for the good old days and somehow obtained Victor's blessings to play them out. Maybe what rakes me most is that this new *Full Metal Jacket* world order has more restrictions than Talonswood Reform imposed *before* Victor loosened the strings. Asher isn't returning us to what's worked, he is herding us into his own version of military paradise.

The magic inside me tickles as it shifts, the now-familiar image of Asher's fiery ass forming with a question. I can't imagine Kitten understood any of the fae's edicts, but maybe something about my emotions gave him a hint. Interesting. With more effort than it should take, I shake a mental *no* toward the image and feel tingles of regret shimmer through my magic as it dissolves.

The following days follow the same pattern. A blazing alarm calls the school to formation at the ass crack of dawn, Asher informs us of something appropriately menacing, and then we run. A lot. The rest of the day is split three ways between academics—the only hint that Asher still believes he's running a school, not a regiment—physical training, and Asher's new invention of work details organized around putting the Academy back to rights after the attack's damage.

"Do you get a sense we're being punished for being attacked?" I ask Mika on our Thursday morning run as the whole cohort of first year cadets stampedes through the forested trail. She's fresh as a daisy in her blue training uniform, black hair pulled up in a topknot, with tiny wisps falling around her round cheekbones. With no change to her breathing and not a single drop of sweat marring her pale skin, she may as well be out on a gentle stroll. A fact that used to bother me a lot more. At least now I can finish most runs, instead of falling on my face before the mile mark. I'm not nearly as fast as the demis, but I'm proud to say that I no longer feel like a corgi trying to keep up with greyhounds.

"Somewhat." My friend lowers her voice. "But I might have accidentally come across some message traffic that says the council is preparing an inspection. So I think it's more about Asher and Victor needing to look good before their higher-ups."

"Great." I close my eyes for a moment, a familiar nauseating déjà vu rippling through me. The one thing you learn never to underestimate in foster care is what the people above you are willing to do to please the people above *them*. Sometimes it means splurging on new clothes for your empty wardrobe right before inspection. Other times, it's a beating from hell to remind you to behave. And it's not looking like Asher and Victor are much interested in new clothes.

"Samantha." Reese's British accent brushes my cheek, and I realize the vampire has joined the morning jog, his booted feet landing against the packed dirt with easy precision. He's shucked his usual all-black today in favor of a long-sleeved forest-green base layer, the sweat-wicking fabric hugging his muscles as if tailor-made for him. His black hair is in a low knot, highlighting his sculpted jaw and cheekbones, full lips, and piercing blue eyes. It's not fair that someone so large should run so easily, but Reese seems as much at ease on the narrow, shadowed trail as he might lounging on the couch.

Without blinking an eye, Mika quickens her pace, giving us some privacy. I've learned that tact around the males and me is one of her many superpowers.

The other cadets are already far ahead, their blue uniforms disappearing quickly through the dense green forest. And all of a sudden, I'm alone with Reese and birdsong. After having kept his distance for several days, the vampire's appearance at my side catches my body utterly unprepared.

Heat races through me at once, my thighs tingling with the memory of the many, many things the male is capable of doing to me. The things that make me wet even as my mind screams at the wrongness of my enjoyment. As Reese's sea-breeze scent washes over me, it's all I can do not to reach out and brush my fingers along his cool skin, as if that might chase away the emptiness inside me.

Which is a cosmic joke given that until now, the vamp has made zero attempts to talk to me since this whole thing with Asher started. Apparently, knowing that Ellis is gone, that there will be no Cassis and his soul-moving piano waiting for me at next liberty, and that I've been pulled away from my one friend and relocated to a glorified dungeon weren't good enough reasons for Reese to seek me out.

The back of my mind whispers that Asher had very likely ordered Reese to stay away from me just as he'd ordered Ellis to. New rules, heightened discipline, and all that. But the greater, less rational part of me doesn't care. Even if Asher ordered Reese to stay away, Reese is still the one blindly *following* the directive to the fullest.

"Are you all right?" he asks in a low, gravelly voice.

"Does it matter?" Fuck. I sound like a weak little girl. "I'm not happy with the new regime." There, truth without petulance.

"I understand."

"If you sounded any more sympathetic, I'd worry there was an imposter taking residence inside your body," I say.

Reese runs on, keeping pace with me with such effortless ease that it gets slightly annoying. Not that I'm under any delusions about ever outrunning him, but it still rubs me the wrong way that my hard-won endurance is nothing but child's play in his world.

"I don't believe making you happy was one of the goals of the recent changes," Reese says after a few beats. His beautiful face is as calm and impossible to read as always, even as he swats away a low-hanging pine branch.

I stumble, pulling my hand out of his reach as he tries to steady my elbow. Because, what the actual fuck?

"I never said it should be." I quicken my pace—which is, of course, useless, but at least makes me feel like I'm doing something. "You asked me whether I was all right. I'm not sure what answer you were expecting, Reese."

A frown flickers across his face. "Truthfully, neither do I," he says after a moment. "Samantha… I realize it may not seem like it now, but your enrollment in Talonswood Reform is simply a temporary inconvenience that will be over in a few years. Once you graduate, you will be free to make your own choices—well, freer. Given the problem of physical separation between you and me—and possibly Ellis and the others—we will need to coordinate our movements. Until then, this remains the safest and most advantageous arrangement for your placement—even if there was a choice about it. Which there is not."

Coordinate our movements. Advantageous arrangement for placement. The male sounds like a fucking educational recording and not someone who's made me come over and over until I screamed myself hoarse.

I snort at myself. What did I expect exactly when we all agreed about sex just being sex? Somehow, between getting snatched from New Jersey and today, I've managed to forget that no one owes me a damn thing. No one.

"Now that I think about it, you're right, sir," I tell Reese, focusing my attention on a messy-branched tree a few hundred yards out in order to break the long run into smaller, more manageable chunks. "That sounds like a reasonable plan."

I quicken my pace another notch, purposely driving myself to a point where breathing, much less talking, is no longer feasible. Maybe I'm a coward to escape Reese this way, but I'm a coward who is stopping being an idiot very quickly.

"Samantha." Reese's hard voice pierces through my self-made shield of gasping breath and pounding feet.

I ignore him. Shove him utterly from my mind.

It's only when I see Reese slam into a tree that I realize I didn't just shove him from my thoughts. I shoved him, period. With my magic.

9

ASHER

*a*sher rested his forearm on the windowpane, watching the cadets hurry across the green toward the training sands under a drizzling late-fall rain. At his orders, the guards had set out piles of logs, which the cadets would carry in teams through an obstacle course for afternoon training. If all went as planned, it would be a miserable few hours that would leave the first years too tired to do anything but crawl to dinner.

"I'd say your goal of becoming the Academy's most hated creature is working like a bloody charm." Settling on the couch behind him, Reese poured Asher a glass of whiskey from the decanter and filled a silver cup with blood for himself. The vamp looked…strained. Vamps and fae little liked being separated from their mates. Asher shook himself mentally—Ellis and Reese should have considered the ramifications of mating before undoing their flies.

"Is it everything you were hoping it to be?" Reese prodded him.

"Mmm. That and more." Asher started to push away from his observation post, his gaze stumbling upon the witch at just

55

the wrong moment. If Samantha had been stunning when she first arrived at Talonswood, the extra strength and endurance work had turned her figure breathtaking. Watching the wind ruffle through her hair, which still had rebellious red streaks that shimmered in the with raindrops, Asher felt his cock twitch painfully. Of course, none of this was new. His damn body deferred to neither reason nor common sense when it came to the witch, and no matter how furious that made him —and it made him damn fucking furious—there was nothing to be done for it except endure the pressure that was Sienna's last laugh.

The long-dead witch had somehow engineered the horsemen's physical attraction to Samantha, even laid all the groundwork for the mating bonds to snap into place. But even with Sienna's great power, the crucial steps still remained within everyone's personal control. A mating bond couldn't snap in without sexual consummation.

Good thing no male had ever died of a tight cock.

Plus, Asher and Victor had an agreement, and Asher was not going to sacrifice the well-being of the Academy—and of Samantha herself—for an orgasm.

"Asher?" Reese prompted. "Should I take this blood to go?"

What had the vamp been asking? Asher walked over to the couch and picked up his drink, knowing better than to expect the whiskey to take the edge of. At least it gave his hands something to do.

"I asked how exactly we were defining success under this new regime of yours," said Reese.

"The way Talonswood Reform has always defined success: cooperation between creatures, demonstration of self-discipline, and a bone-deep understanding of what is and is not acceptable behavior in the world at large," Asher said with more assertiveness than he'd meant to. Reese was a friend, and Asher well knew that wasn't what the vamp was really asking.

"Since kicking this off about a week ago, I've broken up exactly two fights between the creature factions—down from what was getting to be two a fucking day under Victor's former rules," Asher added in a more appropriate tone. "And even those two stayed at the level of bruises and bloody noses instead of attempted murder, which I barely pulled Christian from committing in the wake of the attack. I've handed out half as many lashes as last month, and for all the cadets' complaining, none of it is about creatures being treated differently."

"Only about brutality."

"Really, Reesand?" Asher cocked a brow, trying and failing to understand what the vamp was on about. They both knew that when it came to that particular term, Asher had nothing on Reese. Asher's military expertise had centered around making large forces battleworthy, not honing the skills of elite special-forces warriors. Even striking subordinates, which had gone out of style among mortals a few centuries ago, didn't hold a candle to the self-inflicted broken bones that Reese's training regularly resulted in.

In fact, if Asher recalled correctly, the last time the American SEALS—or was it the British SAS—had Reese in their instructor cadre, he'd marched a company of trainees so hard that two-thirds of the poor bastards had a dozen stress fractures in their feet before the trek was half over. And when Reese found out, he'd kept marching them anyway.

Reese was no kinder to his own body—perhaps even worse —since his vampiric physiology could endure more punishment.

Except something in Reese had changed lately. A steadiness, an occasional lightness slipping through the black cloud that had clung to him ever since Sienna murdered his wife.

"I never said I agreed with the cadets' assessment," Reese drawled. "Nor do I give a bloody fuck whether they believe that Talonswood Reform is catering to them appropriately."

"Then what exactly is your point with this conversation?" Asher regretted the question as soon as he voiced it. He didn't want to know Reese's point. In fact, all Asher wanted just now was an icy shower to ease the pressure that *still* gripped his balls, and maybe a good hard run after that. Maybe he'd even join the log carry, so long as he could do it without bumping into the witch and setting his cock off again. Sienna might have forged Asher's physical attraction to Samantha, but fortunately, Asher had the brains and willpower to overcome the pull.

"My point is you." Putting down his drink, Reese leaned toward Asher, muscled forearms braced on his knees. "You've been at this game for centuries. Shaping armies, captaining vessels, whipping groups of delinquent demis into decent creatures who can be trusted not to start World War III with the humans. Unifying people toward the greater good of the world. You know what all those worthy endeavors have in common?" Reese raised a hand, extending fingers as he spoke. "First, they let you define your own life exclusively by how well you can make *other people* achieve goals. And second... Second, you get to always be alone. The general alone in a tent, the captain keeping distance from his crew, the commander all the Talonswood cadets can collectively hate. When does it end, Asher?"

"Never." A blaze of heat that had been rising inside Asher with every one of Reese's words now spilled into his blood. Suddenly no longer interested in the whiskey, Asher slammed the glass down onto the table and got to his feet, stalking toward the door.

Reese stepped in front of the door, blocking Asher's way, his chest expanded under his black crewneck. He had Asher by a couple of inches, but Asher had him in rank—something Reese sorely needed reminding of right now.

"Move," Asher said simply.

"We've all taken different paths since Sienna," Reese said into Asher's face, not backing away a single inch. "And I know a damn thing or two about punishing myself over and over and bloody over for being the one who lived. For getting caught in the first place, for not fighting hard enough or smart enough. I didn't even see the extent of the darkness I was spiraling through, not until now. And I'm telling you, you are just as blind as I was."

"I said, move," Asher repeated.

"Something has changed," Reese said instead. "I feel things again. And so does Ellis—the brother who hid for centuries in Talon's shadows but has now stepped into the light to be with a witch. You need to—"

"You like Ellis's fucking choices? Then go have your chat with him." Asher's heart was pounding now, the fury echoing though his bones. Who the hell did Reese think he was, telling Asher that everything he'd built over the centuries didn't live up to some new irrelevant metric? Slamming his palm against the door behind Reese's shoulder, Asher leaned forward to bring his face close to the vamp's. To remind the lieutenant exactly who answered to whom.

"You want to talk about Sienna?" Asher snarled into Reese's face. "Let's talk about Sienna. About how I'm the only one of the four horsemen to have continued the mission we started with. Did you forget about peace between species? Coexistence that doesn't involve hunting each other down? I haven't. So you know what I've been doing while Ellis drowned himself in our father's dirty work? While you gorged on a buffet of special forces torment? While Cassis said fuck it, and bought himself all the women, wine, and song he could handle? I was here. Teaching demis to work together, giving them a chance to live beside humans and each other. So don't you fucking tell me that I don't have my shit together. Now, is there anything else I can clear up for you, *Lieutenant*?"

Reese held Asher's stare for one more short heartbeat before dropping his eyes, the years of training and discipline finally taking hold. "No, sir."

"Are you sure?" Asher demanded, anger pulsing through him in rhythm with his heart. "You seemed to have had a nice chat with our resident witch during the morning run. Maybe there is some nugget of wisdom you've dug up there too?"

Reese's jaw tightened, but his gaze remained on the floor. "I asked Samantha how she was faring. I didn't realize that violated protocol."

"It doesn't." Asher shoved away from the door—and Reese —in disgust. "So long as you check in and see every other damn cadet is doing just as well. In fact, maybe you should get on that, Lieutenant. Now. You are dismissed."

10

SAM

y dungeon room does not come with its own bathroom, so my Saturday morning starts with a trek up to what must have been the guards' locker room when this place was in regular use. Fortunately, my room is only a short set of stairs away. There's a damp, rock-walled corridor that leads in the other direction as well, farther underground into rooms that I never ever want to see.

By the time I've showered and taken Kitten out for his morning flight—thankfully, the dragon is naturally opposed to taking a dump where we sleep—I'm more than ready for breakfast and the first day of liberty under Asher's new regime.

I hold the cell door open for Kitten as he flies back in beside me. While the dragon isn't allowed inside any nondungeon building, he's gotten so good at begging for celery that he usually manages to coerce someone into sneaking some out for him from the kitchens. I have no idea why celery.

Sprawled on his back on the bed, Kitten blinks sleepily at me.

"Really? You are the laziest dragon I've ever met," I inform the beast.

He opens one yellow eye, and I can almost imagine him saying, *and how many dragons have you met, exactly?* Then again, maybe that looks means *can I have pineapple-flavored magic when you get back?* Who knows?

My hand curls around the iron bars making up the fourth wall of my room as I suddenly wonder what Janie, the girl who's been as close to a little sister as I've ever had, would say if she knew I have a dragon. A fire-breathing celery-loving dragon. Janie's always wanted a pet. I think all of us foster kids did. There was never a damn chance of that of course. Hard enough to find people willing to take on a little brat without also dragging a dog along. Who cares about the orphans having one living creature in their lives who loves them unconditionally? Yeah.

My throat tightens, and I make myself stop thinking of that. Ellis promised that the money Janie was to receive in exchange for my coming here, was placed in an account for her under the auspices of a scholarship for the essay she supposedly submitted. Whatever else, Janie has a roof over her head and food. That's always been good enough for me.

So why do I now crave more?

Walking into the mess hall, I spot Mika waving me over from a corner table and sit myself down beside her and a box of cereal. Around us, the large room is abuzz with conversation, the circular tables filled with cadets of all years, all dressed casually for liberty in designer jeans and clingy $150 T-shirts that show off their perfect immortal bodies. I adjust my leather jacket—old, but utterly mine. Just like these hair-too-small black jeans with the hole in one knee. "How's it going?" I ask.

The petite demi looks at me through her entirely

unnecessary oversized teal glasses, and I swear I see her eyes lined with red. Shit. It's not that demis—and full vamps, for that matter—can't cry, but their bodies tend to operate on reduced power so it takes a significant stimulus to get actual tears. And now I notice her clothes—a baggy gray sweatshirt and pink flannel pajama pants that are unraveling at the bottom. About as far from her usual bright, formfitting geometric San Francisco fashion as she could possibly get. My stomach tightens, my gaze already sweeping the room to find whoever it is that hurt her.

Mika's eyes follow mine, as if scanning for listening posts. "Asher threw a surprise inspection at one in the fucking morning last night. Our entire floor then spent about three hours on hands and knees stripping and waxing the floor by hand. You're lucky you aren't bedding down with us anymore."

I give her a dark look.

"Well, maybe not." Mike sinks lower in her chair. "I've picked up some more chatter about this whole New World Order. It sounds like the council is planning to send evaluators here in one month—well, three weeks now. So Asher is polishing up his boots for inspection. Us being the boots in the analogy."

Three weeks. No wonder Asher suddenly has such a long rod up his ass. My stomach rumbles, and I gulp down my cereal, my childhood instincts taking over. Never put off for later what you can get now. Especially food.

Which is why I also notice the lack of food going into Mika's mouth, the piece of toast in her hand more of a toy than nourishment. Mika usually has a thing for crunchy toast, like Kitten's obsession with celery. Not to mention there's no way in hell she was crying over a work detail when she barely sleeps normally.

"What's wrong, really?" I lean toward her, playing back her words, putting them together with what I know of Mika. "And when you say *I hear*," I add suspiciously, "how exactly did you happen to—"

"I hacked into Victor's emails," she says quickly, her face dark. "It's a nervous habit. And there was nothing interesting in that account anyway. A bunch of warnings from the council that if everything isn't tip-top bibbity-bop when they show up, they're going to reexamine who is running this place."

"And you got caught?" I ask. That kind of hacking is what landed her here to begin with.

"On that? No. It was toying with the locks, making the little lights play "Jingle Bells" at lights out. Which isn't something I was even trying to hide, because the damn things are about as easy to hack as a child's toy car—why would someone put more effort into tracking interference with the system than securing it to begin with?" Mika's words drop so low that I can barely hear. "But Asher said they'd run a diagnostic and found the signal tampering had come from my room and… It seems I'd crossed some line in his mind."

My hands curl around the edge of the table. "Did he beat you?" I demand quietly.

Mika shakes her head, her big brown eyes filling with tears —which makes my blood start to pound painfully in my temples. "I begged him to do that," she whispers. "I got on my knees and begged. But he wouldn't. He…he took my computer."

I blink. "We can get it back."

She shakes her head again, black hair falling out of her scrunchie. "He took it and put a big-ass magnet right across the top. There's no coming back from that. And then he saw my backup drive, and he put the magnet right on that as well. It's all I have. Had."

Rage. Unmitigated rage flows through my blood as I squeeze Mika's wrist. For Mika, losing her computer is like losing family, and only an idiot could spend one second with her and not know that.

And Asher is no idiot. I think he knew exactly how much she cared about that thing, and exactly what he was doing when he destroyed it.

"On your feet!" Asher's voice fills the mess hall as the male in question walks in, hands behind his back. I hate how panty-soaking beautiful the asshole is, his straight back, broad shoulders, and angled jawline rivaling Hollywood's action heroes. But there's more too. Command vibrates from him, filling the room and making my skin tingle. Making my own body feel like a betrayal.

I spring to my feet with the others, glad to have something to do to relieve the unwelcome tension inside my core.

"You've not earned your liberty," Asher announces, his cool gaze sweeping the vast, raftered room in challenge. A few gasps and murmurs ripple through the space, quickly silenced by two hard claps from Asher. Even in silence, the discontent in the mess hall is thick enough to cut—not that Asher cares. "This morning, everyone is to return to work in detail. You may make up your own teams, so long as each grouping has a representative of at least two species. Depending on my satisfaction with the morning's progress, I will make a decision about the rest of the day. Now, you are dismissed. Breakfast is finished."

After years of experience, my first thought is self-congratulation for having swallowed my cereal when I had the chance. My second is about how much I despise the fucking asshole.

"Hey, Sam-Witch." Standing over our table with his hands in the pockets of his distressed Diesel jeans, Christian has a black silk bandana covering his damaged eye, one piece of thick brown hair falling over it rakishly, and a stance that's as cocky as ever. Behind him, Leanne and several of the other Christian cronies wait in quiet ambush. "Join our team."

I snort. "Find someone else for target practice. I've got places to be and rubble to move from one fucking pile to another."

Christian shifts his weight, his head dipping slightly. "I mean it. Look, I don't claim to have liked you very much, but if you hadn't been around, a whole lot more of us would have been dead when the wolves came." His French accent makes the *r* roll musically. "So… I've reconsidered."

"Idiot," Leanne mutters behind Christian.

Spinning around faster than I can follow, Christian grabs the girl's long black hair and slams her to the floor beside my feet. "Apologize," he hisses to her. "Now."

Leanne swallows and, to my utter blasted shock, does not go off on a tirade about my likely lineage. "My apologies. I would… I would be greatly appreciative if you joined our work team today."

Christian snorts and looks back up at me. "Obedience is faster than sincerity, but I'm working on it." He sighs, his voice actually sounding like a normal being for once. "Come on, Sam-Witch. You need to be on someone's team, and if you're not with us, we'll have to take a wolf, and we all know that will just end with more quality time with Asher. Your friend is welcome too. Whatever you think of us, we are at least good at lugging heavy things around."

I exchange glances with Mika. I trust Christian as far as I can throw him, but he's right—we don't have many options. If this invite is a trap, well…any other could be just as much of one.

After pulling lots with the other teams, we end up with the

science-building assignment, which is a bit ironic given that I had a significant hand in destroying the thing. The feel of Asher's eyes on me when Christian presents our work party detail to him is unsettling, though. As if he doesn't trust this alliance of ours. Then again, everything about Asher is unsettling.

We're two hours into carrying out pieces of the science building—something a machine could do twice as efficiently in half the time—when Christian grabs hold of a twisted metal beam that keeps getting in our way.

"Christian," I shout, my eyes widening as I realize he's about to heave the thing loose. "You can't—"

"Want to fucking bet?" he snarls, his head bleeding where he just smacked it against the offending beam for the third time today. Dust hangs so thick in the air that, despite the morning sun, it's hard to see what we're doing.

"No! I mean—" I cut off. *What I mean* is suddenly all too clear. With an angry screech, a slab of stone above our heads drops a few inches, shifting precariously on its new perch. My body freezes, not knowing which direction to leap. The ominous sound comes again, from the top and right and everywhere. My heart pounds, the world slowing, each deadly fraction of a second unfurling before me. The creak of metal and stone. Leanne's open mouth and pointing finger. Mika's pale terror-filled face.

I inhale a lungful of choking dust.

Cristian releases the metal beam, but it's way too late. As quickly as the world slowed, it starts up again in a shower of deadly concrete.

11

SAM

I shove my hands toward the falling stones. It's absurd. As absurd as raising a palm to shield against flying bullets. But I can't help myself, it's instinct. Just as the energy coalescing inside me is instinct, magic that's rushing from me. The way it rushed at Ellis. And Reese. Except now, it's heading for a hail of deadly slabs.

I feel a force ricochet through me as the slabs of stone and concrete slam down on the invisible shield of my magic and fall harmlessly in a ring around us. The shield flashes out of existence as quickly and instinctively as it materialized. Christian, Leanne, Mika, and I rush out of the danger zone, the two other vamps on the team pulling us the last step of the way. I collapse to my knees on the grass, my heart pounding so hard that the world sways. My lungs hurt, the dust and quick breaths making it hard to draw enough oxygen.

"Holy fucking shit," Christian pants, his hands on his thighs, olive skin flushed with adrenaline. "Not bad, Sam-Witch."

"Unless she orchestrated the whole thing to begin with."

Leanne's once-navy-blue blouse is covered with soot as she glares at the collapsed work site. "You know how much work it will be to get this re-sorted? Maybe she should have thought of that before directing her fucking magic to break even more shit."

I'm too tired to argue, but apparently, Christian is not. "She was in there with us, Leanne. Why would she have sabotaged the very site she was standing in?"

"How the fuck would I know? Why was she standing around naked in the middle of the green when the wolves came. No, sorry, not naked—in nothing but Lieutenant Reesand's shirt. You'll forgive me if I don't trust a slut who spreads her legs for every man in power."

I wait for Leanne's words to wash fury over me, but they don't. There is only a bone-deep weariness. "If you're worried about me seducing Count Victor, he's all yours." I rub my hands over my face. "Fuck. In fact, if you're certain that sucking cock gets anyone a reprieve, maybe you can service Asher too. I certainly want nothing to do with the asshole."

"What, do the brothers not come as a pair?" Leanne places special emphasis on the word *come*.

"If they did, maybe I wouldn't be bedding down in a fucking dungeon." I climb to my feet and dust myself off. I don't know why Leanne is so insistent on trying to get under my skin, or why Christian isn't. But I'm tired. As for Leanne's juvenile slut shaming? That shit only has as much power as people give it, so I decide to go with straight-up reality.

"I had sex with Ellis, if that's what you're wondering," I say lazily. "And Reesand too, by the way. If I wanted to have sex with Asher, the last thing in the world that would stop me is your opinion about it, Leanne. That said, the only thing I'd actually like to do with that asshole is cut off his balls and stick them down his throat so far that he can't take a shit."

Christian snorts in amusement, then his face hardens, though it's difficult to make out facial expressions with his one eye covered. "I'm under orders to be…nice."

"You need orders to not tempt the wrath of a male who can have you picking acorns off the green for ten hours straight?" I ask.

Christian glares at the debris we just escaped from. "Not Asher. You. Count Victor ordered me to be nice to you. Not that I don't appreciate the save, but…" His jaw works as if he's chewing something. "I think Asher has something on the Count. Why else would I be told to make nice with a witch instead of enforcing the proper respect Victor is due? Whatever Asher has on him, it's making Count Victor back away from the demivamps he came here to observe. I don't like it. And if you're telling the truth about your feelings for Asher, Sam-Witch, then—"

"Shut up, Christian." Leanne plants herself in front of the vamp, her green eyes flashing, dark hair flying in the wind. "You don't know the witch's allegiance. What would have gotten any of us lashed has gotten her cock. Whatever the witch says, she's in with the fucking fae. You want to take Asher down? Take down the witch."

"No," says Christian.

Ignoring them both, I walk over to Mika, who has her arms wrapped around herself and is rocking back and forth. The girl's black hair is covered with the same thick gray dust as our clothing, her teal glasses broken. "You all right?" I ask quietly.

"Yes," she says, though her head is shaking the opposite direction, her voice barely on this side of shattering. "I don't know why Victor ordered Christian to be nice, though."

"Why is that upsetting?" I ask.

"Because if I had my computer, maybe I could have

checked. Gotten into some account. Been…useful. I don't know any more about Kitten either. And I don't know why he likes celery. Or how big he'll get. Or whether there's something you really need to know and…" A tear slides down Mika's cheek.

I wrap my arms around her, my fury at Asher pounding with hot, hot flares. I don't like tyrants and bullies. Especially gorgeous narcissistic ones who think themselves God's gift to the world. Magic bubbles inside me again, reminding me that I'm not some weakling who needs to hide in shadows to survive now. Not anymore.

"Taking me down is stupid." My voice is emotionless as I give Mika one final squeeze and stride back to where Christian and Leanne are still arguing. "Been there, done that. The definition of insanity is doing the same thing over and over again while expecting a different result." I dust off my leather jacket, feeling my spine straighten. "The way to deal a blow to someone like Asher is to go after something he cares about."

The vamps look at me warily.

"That presumes Asher actually cares about something," Christian says. "And even if he does, it seems to have escaped your notice that we are on a damn island, cut off from everything. Ergo, we've no way to get our hands on whatever *it* is."

I step toward Christian, even though it means I have to tip my head up to look at him. "Tyrants don't care about things. They care about their power. We find a weak spot, something that takes away his agency, and we can give the asshole what he deserves."

The vamp backs up a step, though I don't think he realizes that he's done so. "Maybe we can get him thrown out of the Academy altogether," says Christian. "Show him up in front of the council."

I shrug. I don't care what's done, so long as it puts an end to the bullying.

A smile that has nothing kind in it touches Christian's face. "I still don't like you, witch. But I dislike Asher more."

"Then you're smarter than you look," I tell him, the anger inside me settling into a low simmer. "Now excuse me. Kitten is getting antsy."

THAT EVENING AT DINNER, I can't bring myself to look at Reese, who is sitting beside Asher on the other side of the mess hall. Unlike the interrupted morning meal, dinner is subdued with everyone either too tired or too wary of attracting Asher's wrath to risk bringing attention to themselves. I don't know how Reese would react if he learned of my little speech this morning, but given that he's sitting with Asher and not with me, I have an idea of where his loyalties lie. Not that he owed me anything different. No one does.

The simmering magic inside me, buzzing about like a tiny swarm of bees, is an on-again-off-again companion. Connecting with Ellis and Reese was the spark that brought it to the surface, and the more I use it, the stronger I think it's becoming. Or maybe it's Kitten's presence. Or both. Whatever is happening, I'm not a weak little girl anymore.

My pocket vibrates, and I carefully pull out my phone to check messages. My hopes of remote contact with Ellis have been squashed by the combination of no reception in my dungeon and the male's inability to comprehend that texts don't always have to be about logistical instructions or reminders to keep my hands up in boxing. Cassis, however, faces no such handicap. Expecting to see another inappropriate meme about mating wolves, I'm caught off guard by the message.

Can you come to Dusk tonight? Need your help.

My chest tightens. In all the time I've known Cassis, he's never asked for help. Never phrased anything as a polite request either. A *get your preferably skanky ass to my bar* I could have ignored, but this…? I shift the screen enough to let Mika see the message, her face darkening.

"You can't go off campus," she whispers quickly. "And he shouldn't be asking you to break the rules."

"Cassis hasn't met a rule he hasn't broken," I murmur back, "and I doubt he knows we've had a…fucking culture shift around here. Of course I'm going."

"And if you get caught?" Mika whispers.

"Then I get caught. Catch some punishment. Go on with life." I tighten my jaw, the discussion with Christian and his cronies coming back to me. "Bullies have only the power we give to them. The day I let a tyrannical asshole stop me from helping a friend is the day I stop deserving friends to begin with."

12

SAM

It's eleven at night when I slide into Cassis's convertible, Kitten hopping onto the leather backseat and huffing a bit of smoke. The vamp's gaze narrows on the dragon, one dark brow raised. I sent him a photo, but it isn't quite the same as seeing the little stinker in the flesh. I buckle in and close my eyes at the sweet scent of temporary freedom.

Around us, the night sky is filled with stars, deep shadows playing across Cassis's sharply carved features. I waited until after the Academy was buttoned down for the evening before leaving, taking the same route as the first time I snuck out. It was just as easy, which makes me wonder if Asher isn't tempting people into disobedience to get an excuse to torment them.

"Asher is going to skin you alive if he finds out you left campus," Cassis says by way of greeting, as if he weren't the one who asked me to come in the first place. I don't hold it against him, though—it's the vamp's way of giving me a chance to change my mind and back out. He jerks his chin toward Kitten, a flurry of thoughts flashing behind his piercing eyes before his face settles back into its unfazed self, as if extinct creatures were a common occurrence in his life. "And I'm going to do the same to that lizard if he melts my seats."

"I'm not worried," I say. "Well, except about your seats. I know your priorities, and it's more than anyone's life is worth to leave a scratch. Kitten, take note."

"Sassy. I don't know whether this new you makes me want to have wild sex or run for cover." His rich British tones brush against my skin, biologically calculated to make his prey swoon —and I nearly do. Cassis puts his hand on the clutch but doesn't yet shift gears to get us into motion. He's stalling. "I'm serious, Samantha. I've been so busy with a snatcher mess that I didn't realize Asher's been tightening ship until after I texted."

"For the second time, I'm not scared of Asher." It feels good to say it. Feels good to breathe in Cassis's scent of spice and sin and watch the wind play through his thick dark hair, catching the tips of his black silk Tom Ford lapels. My magic stretches, yawning happily. "If the asshole catches me, I'll deal with it. So there you go."

"If I knew you enjoyed pain, Samantha, I'd have set up my bedroom in preparation," Cassis purrs, shifting the car into Drive with his usual lithe grace that belies his broad shoulders and thickly muscled torso. The male truly has the kind of body that would give any underwear model an inadequacy complex. "Whatever that overgrown beagle can do, I know I can do better."

I cut my eyes to Cassis, admiring the perfection of his silhouette against the star-filled sky. Deliciously untouchable.

"Don't get your hopes up. I *don't* like pain." Of course, the moment the words are out of my mouth, my mind leaps to the too-erotic-for-fairness spanking that Reese unleashed on my defenseless ass. The pinkest elephant of all thoughts. I clear my throat, tumbling ahead before the male can catch the change in scent. "What's a snatcher mess?"

Cassis frowns in disgust. "Snatchers is a term from centuries ago for pricks who take humans on a one-way trip to Talon. The kind with a lifetime employment guarantee."

My breath freezes. "Are you saying the fae have been running a slave operation for a few hundred years?"

"Of course they have." Cassis shoots me a *don't be naïve* glance. "Oh, it's not *all* fae, just a dark syndicate here and there. It's highly illegal, but it happens. Inconveniently, it's been happening too often of late—and it's starting to interfere with my business. Not to worry, though. I'll get it sorted."

Right. Why would I worry about that? "Well, if I'm not here to chat about mass kidnapping, what did you need?"

"Your company."

I cock a brow.

"I missed you." He bats his lashes, barely watching the road as he speeds neatly through the narrow streets of downtown Talonswood.

"Lovely," I say, forcing my hand to loosen its grip on the cup holder.

Low brick storefronts rise on all sides of us now, shuttered for the night, their second-floor apartments glowing cheerily from within. Cassis pulls into the cobblestone street in front of his club, stopping so suddenly that Kitten flaps his wings with a small screech, barely managing to stay on the seat.

I glance toward the glowing sign above Dusk, my chest tightening. I've missed this place. The piano. I've missed Cassis. "Well, if you need time to beat around the mental bush, I'll start the evening by getting drunk."

Cassis opens the glove compartment and hands me a flask.

I snort, opening the top and taking a careful sniff. Whiskey. The very expensive kind, if I know my friend.

"What have I missed at Dusk?" I ask, taking a small taste, warmth spreading exquisitely into my chest.

"The good strippers, better alcohol, and somewhat questionable patronage," Cassis hops out, not bothering with the car door. Now that we're here, there's a tightness to the vamp's movements. A discomfort I haven't seen before. And if it's not a syndicate of kidnappers hindering his steps, then what the hell is?

Kitten bounces over to my shoulder, suddenly alert to all the delicious noises coming from inside. Curiosity flows in the bond between us, the little dragon clearly excited to go inside and…and taste things?

"No," I tell him, glaring into golden eyes. "No biting the guests. Or the furniture."

Kitten blinks his innocence, the tip of his tail tapping against my leather jacket. Wisps of buzzing magic take another—very familiar shape. Long and semicircular. Celery.

"Maybe," I promise, catching up to Cassis, who holds the door open for me. We stride into the low, pulsing music and swimming blue lights of Dusk together, the half-naked pole dancers putting an extra twist into their hips as the vamp passes. Cassis grabs a drink meant for someone else from a waitress's tray and takes a hearty gulp as he guides us to an open spot at the bar.

By instinct, I duck under the partition. Even though I'm not working today—at least I don't think I am—there's a familiar pleasure to standing behind the bar. A feeling of belonging that I've missed. My gaze travels lazily over the music and debauchery—and comes to a sharp halt at the corner barstool and the boy of about eight or nine sitting atop it.

"Now that you're here," Cassis mutters, following my gaze. "There's somebody I need you to meet."

The boy, a thin golden-haired kid with tawny eyes, shoots me a dagger-filled glare.

"Right," says Cassis, gesturing between the boy and me. "Jake, meet Sam. Sam, Jake. Sam, Jake is a runaway. Jake, Sam is…well, someone who's better equipped to deal with you than I am. Everyone on the same page? Lovely. Call me when you're done."

13

SAM

I grab Cassis's arm as he tries to escape, yanking the vamp toward me. Or I try to—it's like yanking a tree, the absolute power in his muscles letting me know exactly how outmatched I am. Finally, he gives way, turning into my space with a suddenness that forces me to crane my neck back to look at him.

"When we're done with what exactly?" I demand.

"How am I supposed to know?" Cassis hisses back. "That... *Child thing* just showed up." Detangling from my grasp, Cassis pours a drink for himself and empties it in one gulp. "Everyone I know except you out-ages the little vermin by several centuries. So here you are. And I'd be most obliged if you could make him go away."

"To where?"

"To wherever humans keep the little things until they're old enough to fend for themselves nowadays. I'm not exactly set up to run a daycare." Cassis waves his hand around Dusk, at the sea of skulking, drinking, dancing vamps, the huge screens in the corners highlighting everything in vivid, lurid

81

detail. The video engineer chooses that very moment to zoom in on the curved lines surrounding a stripper's thong.

I rub my face. "Where did you get him?"

"I didn't request him from a mail-order catalogue, Samantha," Cassis says. "He walked in. And sat. And he is still sitting here."

"Actually…he *was* sitting here," I say, staring at the now-empty stool. A moment later, a second thought occurs to me, my shoulder feeling suddenly light. "Where's Kitten?"

"Bollocks." Cassis throws back the rest of his latest drink, and we spread out through the club in a dual search.

As I press between the dancing bodies, that feeling of home washes over me again. When I first came to Dusk, I nearly started a riot. Now, I push full vamps aside with a hurried flick of my hand. And it isn't just because Cassis is close by. I've changed, and the creatures feel it.

A purring sound catches my ear, drawing me toward Cassis's grand piano. My heart stops in horror. Cassis's prized and very burnable wooden piano. Nearly tripping a waitress off her feet, I rush to the instrument's rescue, only to find it both dragon-free and intact.

"There." Coming up beside me, Cassis points beneath the piano, where Jake lies on his belly nose to nose with a fire-breathing dragon.

"Upstairs," Cassis barks to the three of us. "Now."

Jake turns his shaggy blond head, somehow managing to look down at Cassis despite being under a piano and a fraction of the vamp's size. "Who died and made you God?" The boy's British accent catches me off guard.

"A great many people," says Cassis, flashing his fangs. "And I'm more than happy to add a little boy to the list."

Jake pales slightly and crawls out, every line of his body

making it clear that he is obeying under protest. I hold my hand out to Kitten.

The dragon hops promptly onto my shoulder, as if he were some kind of trained pet and not a pain-in-the-ass reptile.

Jake glares at me. "You better give my dragon back, or I'll tell him to melt you to goo."

"*Your* dragon?"

Jake lifts his chin, his T-shirt loose over a too-skinny chest. "Finders keepers."

"I truly hope you're wrong about that." Cassis puts his palm between the boy's shoulder blades and pushes him toward the steps leading to his upstairs apartment. "Because I've absolutely zero desire to keep you."

A few minutes later, Jake and I are sitting on one of Cassis's sleek black couches while the vamp pulls a bench from his baby grand piano—a smaller twin to the one downstairs. Floor-to-ceiling windows give us a perfect view of the glittering lights of Talonswood and the great black expanse of forest beyond. Kitten curls up between Jake and me like a puppy, using his long, spiked tail as a chin rest. He hiccups contentedly, a tiny jet of orange flames skimming over Cassis's Italian leather.

"Can't we muzzle him?" Cassis asks.

I raise a brow. "Do you have a dragon muzzle?"

"I wasn't talking about the reptile," says Cassis.

Jake crosses his arms, his gaze never stopping at any one spot for too long. The boy is smart enough not to trust anyone. It occurs to me suddenly that I haven't seen children anywhere on Talonswood. Certainly not at the Academy. I hadn't thought about it before, but I guess there would be no reason for a child to be on the island. Demis don't come into enough power to attract attention until young adulthood, full vampires come into being as adults, and fae, well, I suppose most choose to raise their young in Talon or concealed among humans.

"Why are you here in Talonswood?" I ask Jake.

He flips me off, which I should have seen coming—that kind of information is too personal to share with strangers. All right, something more straightforward for now.

"Where are you from?" I ask.

The boy weighs me up and down, eyes more golden than brown in the low lamplight. "London." There is a weariness in his eyes that is too old for a nine-year-old, but has a familiar set to it. The kind that lets one foster child recognize another.

"And do you have parents?" I ask, though I suspect the answer.

"No, I got magicked into existence. By a stork. Without sex." Jake puts extra emphasis on the word *sex*. When neither I nor Cassis react, his jaw tightens. "You know, *fucking*. With a *cock* and—"

"Yes, I'm quite familiar with the act," Cassis drawls lazily. "I'm quite good at it, actually."

Jake blinks, and I swallow an absurd chuckle. A hidden island, fae and vampires walking the earth, a fire-breathing dragon—all that the boy takes in stride for some reason, perhaps had been told about somehow. But Cassis's reaction to his choice of language, that shakes the foundation of Jake's world. Nonetheless, I do want to get us back on track.

"Cut the bullshit, Jake." I cross my arms over my chest. "You know what I was asking."

"You shouldn't swear in front of children," says Jake.

"Agreed," said Cassis. "This isn't getting me anywhere closer to knowing what to do with him. Can we box his ears until he starts making sense?"

I ignore both comments and stroke my fingers along Kitten's spine. The boy is all shield and claws and a deep angry loneliness that I understand all too well. "Enough with the tough act," I say quietly. "As you've noticed, the creatures here do a hell of a lot more than swear. And the last thing you want is to be shown the door."

Jake flinches. Yes, I got him there. Getting ripped apart by a vampire, that's mythology. Being put out in the cold— that...*that* is personal history.

I gentle my voice and pull back to something less personal. "You obviously know about creatures. But Talonswood itself is a highly protected secret from the rest of the world, with strict entry policies. How did you get here?"

"Bought a ticket, like everybody else." Jake looks at me like I'm stupid, then sighs and pulls something out of his pocket and hands it over.

It *is* a ticket, with a wind-shaped logo in the upper left corner and a notation that *Flight of Your Dreams Transportation* one-way fares are nonrefundable, with first come, first serve seat assignments. Complementary meal service including soft drinks and house alcoholic beverages are included in the price. Under the destination section, a stamped lettering reads *TWI.*

"Talonswood International," Cassis says, following my gaze. His voice is hard. Displeased. "*Dreams* changed owners a few years back. Not that it ran the tightest ship before, but now it's downright predatory. Even I don't use them anymore if I have any choice in the matter."

I cock my head in question. What the hell would Cassis be using *any* transportation service for? But the vamp is too busy frowning at the ticket to notice. "How did you get hooked up with them?"

Jake shuts his mouth stubbornly.

Cassis looks toward me. "There are several transportation agencies dedicated to bringing creature-employed humans to Talonswood. Documentation requirements are stringent to ensure that the mortals are, in fact, sponsored. But there's one loophole. The council errs on the side of monitoring everyone with creature blood, and Talonswood is the easiest place to do it from. So anyone with creature blood has...let's call it *automatic citizenship*. The council will even pay their way."

"Wait." Jake's face darkens. "You mean I didn't have to pay for the ticket?"

Ah. So the boy is demi—or at least believes himself to be.

The corner of Cassis's mouth twitches. "The less legitimate transport agencies, like *Dreams*, will double bill anyone they can. But more to the current point, their vetting procedures skew toward profit over the truth. That said, bringing a child over is low even for them."

"I'm not a child. I'm nine."

"My mistake," says Cassis.

"All right." I insert myself back into the conversation. "So, for some reason that you're about to tell us, you wanted to get to Talonswood. And then you *somehow* discover *Dreams Transportation* and get yourself a ticket to Talonswood. And then what? You got off the plane and happened to wander into Dusk?"

Jake shrugs a skinny shoulder, suddenly not nearly as confident as he was just minutes ago. "There was a free shuttle into town. Dusk was one of the only places open this late. And it... Well, it seemed like the kind of place I know. My landlady ran one." Jake turns to Cassis, speaking quickly. "I can clean tables better than anyone you have now. And I never forget a drink order. I run messages. I can even..." His face flushes, his shoulders turning in on themselves before he finds some internal fire that makes his chin rise into the air. "I've heard some patrons might like a small kind of partner. If you give me a chance, you'll make a ton of money. Do we have a deal?"

Jake holds out his hand.

Cassis chokes on air. "Did you just ask me to hire you as a Dusk prostitute?"

"Oldest profession in the world," says Jake.

"True enough." Cassis leans forward. "Do you have any experience in what you are proposing?" he asks with admirable neutrality.

My breath stills, my stomach churning as I await the boy's answer.

"No, but I'm smart." Jake clears his throat before puffing out his chest. "And it doesn't seem all that difficult to——"

Cassis actually growls in a strange mix of relief and fury. "You won't be expanding your education here either. I have this rule about anyone having sex in my establishment needing to be taller than the bar."

Jake purses his lips, his hand still in the air. "Well, you should expand your business, then," he says, his tone full of— thankfully ignorant—fierceness. "There is a large client base."

"If any of those clients enter Dusk, they will find themselves dead. And let me tell you, collecting the tab from dead people is not nearly as easy as you imagine." Cassis twists toward me, throwing up his hands. "Do something, Samantha!"

Kitten hops up onto the armrest beside me and hisses at Cassis, the spikes down his back alert and quivering.

Cassis growls right back at him.

"Easy, tigers," I say. "Something like what, Cassis?" I rub my face and turn back to the boy. "All right. So you've been living in some dark London pub, trading your, errr, services for a bed and bowl. If you were…satisfied with your previous employment, why did you leave?"

Jake's hand, which was still extended hopefully out toward Cassis, falls together with his bravado. The desperation around him is so palpable, it echoes through my blood. I rub my cheek against Kitten and savor the warm, raspy feel of the dragon pressing back into me before nudging him to go hop onto the boy's lap. Kitten complies with enthusiasm while I dig a small plastic bag with celery from my pocket and hand a piece to Jake. "These are his favorite."

Jake swallows, his eyes on the food. Fuck.

"Cassis—" I start, but the vamp is already on it, tapping something into his phone before retrieving a box of crackers and three glasses of whiskey from his bar.

"I'm having dinner sent up," he says. "This is an aperitif."

I snatch the whiskey glass Cassis is extending to Jake and replace it with the box of crackers instead, my chest aching as the boy digs in desperately. For the next few minutes, the only sounds filling the room are crunching crackers and Kitten's wet slurps as he destroys the celery. Then Jake speaks, his voice soft. Vulnerable.

"My mum died giving birth to me. I was in and out of some places then, until settling with my landlady a few years ago. I only found out that mum had a safety deposit box a few months ago. My landlady took me to get it 'cause she hoped there was money inside." For a second, Jake's voice takes on a note of pride. "There was a bit, but I palmed it real quick. But beside that, it was just a bunch of papers Mum was keeping. That's where I found out about fae and vampires and stuff. She'd been working in a place that catered to helping creatures relax when she got pregnant. Once she found out, she started trying to figure which client sired me, but never did. She'd had it narrowed it down to three, though. When I told my landlady, she…well, she freaked out. Said she didn't need any crazies and schizos in her place. I didn't have any place to go after that, and Mum seemed sure my father lived in Talonswood. There was a number in her notes. So I called."

Reaching into his pocket, Jake withdraws a carefully folded

piece of paper and shows it to me, never letting go of the page.

I scan down the list of about ten names and descriptions, seven of them crossed out. The three remaining ones have thickly scrawled lines.

Vyl—fae. Dark skin, very tanned. Yellow eyes. Possibly shifts into an eagle.

Thamaris—vampire. Six feet tall and speaks with a Slavic kind of accent.

Dust—fae. Golden hair. Tawny eyes. Wolf? Unknown. Very regimented.

"So one of these gentlemen is your sire," Cassis says as he stands and walks back to his private bar. Taking out a silver decanter of O negative, he pours a little into a cup and strides back, holding the drink out to Jake.

"What's that?" the boy asks suspiciously.

"You tell me," Cassis says.

Jake takes a careful sniff, his whole face scrunching up in horror. He clamps a hand over his mouth as if about to throw up and glares at Cassis. "That's blood, you arsehole."

I shoot a glare at the vamp too. "What the fuck, Cassis?"

The vamp shrugs one massive shoulder and savors the drink the boy just rejected. "I think we can safely cross out Thamaris from your list. You are most certainly not a demivamp."

I shake my head. "Did your mom have any more information on these males? Beyond that they live in Talonswood, I mean?"

"I don't know how many sex clubs you've been in, luv," says Cassis, "but they don't usually collect a DNA swab ahead of time."

Jake ignores him and turns over the sheet. "She drew these pictures. She was a good artist." His attention flickers back to

Cassis, his voice desperate. "I'm good too. I can paint for you. Walls, fences, anything you want."

"I don't have fences," Cassis tells him with a flicker of his beautiful dark eyes. "Though maybe I should get some barbed wire ones."

"Cassis," I snap, my heart pounding as I take in the painstakingly drawn renderings. Jake is right. His mother drew well. Even with many folds of paper, the three profiles staring at me look lifelike. Very fucking lifelike. Especially because I know one of them better than I wish.

Tawny eyes. Fiery golden hair. A military straight posture.

Dust. Not so different from *Ash.*

I look at Jake. Look back at the drawing. Look at Jake again. And suddenly, those deep-set golden-brown eyes are all I can see.

Blood drains from my face. "Cassis. We know Jake's sire."

14

SAM

With Jake fed and settled with Kitten to sleep in Cassis's guest room, the vampire and I return downstairs and settle into a booth. Though I haven't ordered anything, a waitress appears with a glass of cassis liqueur for me and a glass of whiskey for Cassis. My mind races with too many thoughts to put into words. Fortunately, I don't have to say anything just yet since the male's phone—which he must have silenced while we were upstairs—is now erupting in a storm of loud dings, the screen flashing through the blue-tinted dimness.

"Give me a minute," Cassis mutters, his face dark as his fingers fly over the keypad.

"Take your time." I press the heel of one hand into my temple, suddenly fighting back a headache of monstrous proportions. I gesture to his phone. "Is there a problem? I mean, beyond the obvious."

Cassis nods. "A plane carrying some merchandise that's highly valuable to me went missing a few days ago. I've been trying to track it."

"Do I want to know what was in there?" I ask, wondering if this has anything to do with the *snatcher issue* interfering with the vamp's business.

Cassis puts the phone facedown on the table, his penetrating dark eyes reaching too deeply into me. Dusk's shifting blue lights wash like liquid over the black silk of his suit, casting even deeper shadows over his masterfully sculpted face. "I don't know, Samantha. Do you?"

I swallow, a shiver running down my spine. There's a darkness to Cassis, an edge of danger that's always simmering just beneath the surface. If I'm not careful, I'll get drunk on it. On him. It's the first time I'm seeing him since my bond with Kitten, and the twinges of need I've grown used to in the vamp's company are now twisting into a deeper, gnawing desire. One that drives into my bones with every inhale of Cassis's scent. Sin and spice and clean shampoo.

"What are we going to do about Jake?" I ask instead, fighting against my body. My breath hitches, and I cover the slip with a sharp inhale. "Drop him off on the Academy doorstep and let Asher deal with the rest?"

"Sounds like a reasonable plan to me. I'm not exactly tempted to take up the young gentleman's employment offer." Cassis's eyes flash, reminding me that he lived through the time when what Jake spoke of was the normal course of business. "I'll bring him in the morning. Keep you out of it."

I snort without humor. "I think we're past that. With Jake in the picture, there's no hiding that I was here tonight." I force myself to ignore the quick flash of nerves. "Just call him down here. If I'm going to be in trouble, I might as well get the benefit of watching Asher squirm like a worm on a hook."

Cassis puts away his phone, his brown eyes leaving tendrils of heat as they trail over my face. My sex tingles, clenching to relieve the building pressure. Fuck. I'm already wet, and

Cassis's powerful, dangerous stare is only driving my need up and up, my magic stirring the storm of sensation. I imagine this is what an animal in heat feels like. Clearly, my magic isn't the only thing that's changed lately.

I feel…hungry. Hungry for a connection I haven't had since Ellis's goodbye.

Oh, fucking hell on a popsicle stick.

The vampire's nostrils flare delicately, no doubt taking in my arousal. The bastard leans forward, the tip of his tongue caressing his pointed canine. "I can call Asher. But are you sure you want him disrupting the evening?" His voice rumbles through my body, making my breath shallow.

My mouth is dry. My sex pulsing. "Disrupting it from what?" I ask, then hold up a hand before the vamp can answer. I know this game. I've played it enough. And under usual circumstances, I even find it enjoyable. But not today. "Don't tease me, Cassis. Not tonight. My body already feels like a set of fireworks, and if you play with matches and then run away, it will just hurt."

"You would prefer I stick around for the explosion?" For a second, Cassis seems like he's going to reach out to me, and I can imagine the feel of his lips brushing my skin, a phantom type of music playing through the air between us. But then he flashes a too-quick smile and pulls away, as if some surge protector inside him fired to prevent an override. "Samantha," he whispers, looking down at the table before raising his fire-filled gaze to me. "I'm… I'm not like the others. I'm not *good*. I certainly don't serve and protect or educate wayward demis."

My breath grows shallow, my words hitching. "That works out well, then," I whisper, throwing my own self-preservation into the gutter. Reaching across the table, I tangle my hand in Cassis's thick, silky hair, running my teeth over his bottom lip. "Because I gave up on *good* at around ten this morning."

The growls that escape Cassis's chest sends vibrations all the way down to my sex. Reaching across the table, he grips my sides with a strength that is nothing but supernatural. Lifting me from my seat, he spins me so quickly around the short side of the table that momentum arcs my legs in a semicircle. Still gripping my waist, the vamp sets me on the table in front of him, my thighs spread wide on either side of him. My blue uniform skirt has never felt less relevant.

Lounging back in his seat, Cassis pushes my thighs wider apart, my skirt opening the last bit of the way to give him a full view of my moist panties. His dark eyes are hooded, a faint smile quirking his full lips. The high back of the booth shields some of the view, but with me sitting on the table itself, someone is bound to notice.

"Cassis." My fingers dig into his shoulders, the pounding beat of the music and pulsing lights of the dance floor a distant thing. "Upstairs."

"Why in the world would we do that?" Cassis's eyes flash with a danger that makes my blood feel filled with wine. "Are you afraid someone will see me do this?"

With agonizing precision, the vamp runs his finger just inside my panty line. The rough calluses brush my hot skin, making my nails clamp down on his shoulders.

Damn it. I try and fail to slow my breath. Anyone walking by can look over. See me sitting here, my legs spread, my hips working so hard not to grind against the tabletop.

"You are a bastard," I pant.

"Should I stop?" Cassis cocks an eyebrow. "Have you decided you want to be good after all?"

Gauntlet thrown. Damn it. I should have known better than to tempt this particular vampire. Or maybe deep down, I did know. And did it anyway.

"Good is for pricks like Asher," I tell him, my teeth clenched.

"Mmm. Very true." Cassis's hold on my thighs tightens, and he puts his head down between my legs, taking a deep inhale of my scent. His nose is so close to me that its tip brushes against the moist lace of my underwear, sending an electric shock through my already swollen nerve endings.

My face flames. But I hold still. I even make myself smile, just to prove a point.

Just when I think I'm winning this particular bout, I feel something thin and sharp sting the inside of my thigh. Prickles of erotic pain shoot right to my clit, like gasoline poured on embers. With a start, I realize Cassis just bit me, and I barely swallow a moan that *would* have all of Dusk coming over for the show. *Oh fuck.*

A clink of glasses announces a waitress walking by.

Cassis lifts his head, studying my face with predatory enjoyment, his hand still between my legs. One sound from me and the woman will surely turn toward us. Will know exactly what's happening.

Cassis slips two long fingers inside my panties, stroking up and down between my slippery folds. Up and down, with agonizingly slow, steady pressure, always stopping just shy of my clit. Up and down. Again. As patiently and lazily as if he were stroking a cat.

I clamp my mouth shut and think of ice. Close my eyes too, because just the sight of his beautiful, shadowy face is making my blood boil faster.

"What can I get you?" the waitress, just two booths away from us, asks the guests. I don't hear the answer. I don't dare even glance that way in case she sees the lust written all over my face.

Cassis's fingers stop at my opening, my wetness so thick, it must be running down his wrist. A slow leisurely swirl, and then he slips both fingers inside me at once, without letting me adjust to one first. Intuitively knowing that my body can take it. Is starved for it. He starts pumping the fingers in and out of my channel as lazily as before, drawing tiny sighs out of me that I have no control over. Now he moves faster, tapping my G spot on each thrust, clamping a heavy hand on my thigh to still my helpless movements. Just two fingers and he's turning me into a hot mess right here in the middle of Dusk. I'm a fraction away from moaning, writhing my body for more friction, spectators be damned. The thought of how close we are to getting caught magnifies the sensation in every nerve in my body.

"Shall I set off the fireworks?" Cassis murmurs. "I can, you know. Right here. Right now. You seem to need a bit of relief. All you have to do is ask really nicely."

Asshole. Fucking asshole. The thought of coming on a table in the middle of Dusk sets my whole body on fire, and I'm one breath away from begging him to let me do just that.

Except… Except that isn't what I want. I don't want an orgasm. Well, I do, but I want *Cassis* more. And if he thinks I'll give up this easily, he has another think coming.

Baring my teeth, I push myself forward off the table and straddle the vamp's thighs, the seat's soft leather cool beneath my shins. My hands roam his chest, my mouth covering his as I press him into the back of the bench. His body is as hard as I've always imagined, his steel cock pressing into my backside as I grind against him.

I sweep my tongue through his mouth, my magic buzzing in approval of the spicy taste.

A growl rumbles through the male's chest, and the mouth I've been exploring to my heart's content goes hard. Demanding.

Wrapping his fingers in my hair, Cassis plunges his tongue inside my mouth, heedless of my need to breathe. Harsh, punishing strokes rake through me, the predator finally lured from its den. For better or worse.

His elongated canines graze the inside of my lip, then drop dangerously to the sensitive pulse along my neck.

Oh. Fuck. I hold still, terror and excitement rushing through me as Cassis positions his mouth right on my artery. One small move and I know he *will* bite. Not a teasing nip like the one on my thigh, but the real vampiric kind. My sex pulses, my inability to move a single muscle making me feverish with need.

I pant, struggling not to breathe too deeply. Prey caught in a trap. Cassis's delicious smell floods my senses, a primal musk thickening the spice.

His teeth press harder, taking me to the edge of pain. Another wave of sensation rushes through me, anxiety and fear feeding the arousal. If my pulse hits any harder, I will pierce my own neck on the vampire's razor-sharp teeth.

"I warned you, witch, I don't play by the rules," Cassis whispers, and it's all I can do not to collapse against him as his mouth shifts from my neck to my ear. "And I am not good."

I pull away enough to look into his face. There's wildness there, Cassis's usually rare breaths visible in his rising chest. Beneath me, his cock is so hard that it bruises my sex. "What you are is too full of talk," I tell the male. "And unless I haven't made it clear, I'm not frightened off that easily."

CASSIS

*B*loody hell. Cassis's head spun.

He didn't remember the last time he'd lost control, but the witch on his lap was straining everything inside him to the limit. Her big hazel eyes, her lemongrass scent. Her delicious warm mouth back on his, where he'd always wanted it, plundering his with abandon. Cassis wrapped one arm around her waist and tugged her hips even harder against his, the other plunging beneath her skirt. Samantha thought she could play with him and win? Well, they'd see about that.

Before she could do anything else to toy with his limits, he hooked his fingers around the crotch of her panties and yanked. A wet ripping sound filled his ears as the soft material parted beneath his strength like paper. Sam's mouth broke from his with a gasp, her full pink lips open in shock. He grinned. Lifting her up onto her knees, he undid the zipper on his pants with one hand, finally freeing himself beneath her. Relief rushed through him at the easing pressure—only ramping up again as even more blood and need rushed into his twitching cock.

The witch wanted more? Fine.

Positioning himself at Sam's opening, Cassis let her drop, sheathing himself inside her in one hard movement. She made a small, nearly inaudible sound, like a kitten mewing. Her body jerked, her tight, tight channel stretching and pressing around the intrusion, hot and pliable, as anxiety and lust saturated her scent in equal measure. Fuck, she felt good around him.

Too good.

The little witch straightened out her plaid skirt, the only thing beside the top of the table that concealed what Cassis was doing to her. Bloody hell. She had no idea what effect that modesty was having on him, how it teased his need. Maybe if she knew, she'd hide it better.

Holding her slightly above him with one arm, Cassis undulated his hips slowly, working his cock through her slick channel, in and out, her breath growing harsh. The line between ecstasy and discovery was so thin that one too-loud moan or a too-rhythmic creak of the bench would give them away. Arousal flooded Sam's scent. Soon every vampire in here would know precisely what they were doing from her sweet musk alone—but he didn't need to remind her of that. Her eyelids fluttered as he thrust slightly harder, still holding her perfectly still above him, and then she was kissing him again, working his mouth so hungrily, so thoroughly, that he had no choice but to obey.

With every hot swipe of her tongue, he could feel himself losing ground, losing himself in her heady scent, her smooth bare thighs clamped around him.

Well then. Time to up the ante.

One arm tightly around the witch, Cassis put his other

hand on the back of the booth and raised his voice. "Leroy," he called, summoning one of the techs in charge of Dusk's sound system.

Samantha froze, her nails digging into his biceps.

"Sir?" Dressed all in black, Leroy had a radio and earpiece, his eyes surveying everything in the club even as he approached.

"The bass notes do not sound quite right to me," Cassis said, shifting Samantha so that the head of his cock hit that spot inside her that made her whole body go rigid. "What do you think, Sam?"

"Sounds fine to me." The words came in a croak, and the witch turned around to grab for her drink. Cassis liqueur.

"Are you sure that cassis agrees with you, today?" he asked. "I'm sure Leroy wouldn't mind fetching something else you could put inside you instead."

For a second, Cassis thought Sam might spit out the mouthful she'd taken, her channel now spasming around his cock.

"N-no," she managed, her body positively vibrating. She still thought there was a chance Leroy hadn't guessed what was happening, though only someone without vampiric scent could think that.

Taking his arm off the back of the bench, Cassis dropped it beneath the table and slid his fingers up the witch's thigh. Along her drenched folds. Around her clit. "Holding a witch on your lap is an experience," he told Leroy, who stood with his buzzed blond head bowed slightly in a show of deference. "I'd say try it, but given that Samantha is the only witch around, you might have to wait until we discover a few more."

"Yes, sir," Leroy replied with impressive calm, pale blue eyes glued somewhere around the legs of the next table over.

Cassis traced the hood around Sam's clit, his own cock

pulsing in his ears so hard that it was becoming more difficult to keep up the chatter. The witch's muscles were jerking now, her thighs and calves tensing with her efforts to keep still.

Flick. Flick. Flick. Cassis moved his finger right over her clit, watching a bead of sweat drip down from her temple. She was close. So damn close. *Flick. Flick. Flick.*

"Do you hear that bass, Samantha?" Cassis said, now tapping the witch's engorged clit in time to the music. "It sounds off just there. And there again."

"I usually pay more attention to the higher notes," She was panting desperately, her nails digging so hard into his arms, they drew blood beneath his clothes. She was mind-boggling gorgeous in her desire, red-streaked hair flowing wildly around her face, cheek and lips flushed, eyes round and hazy.

He had her. She was completely his. Triumph tugged at the corners of his lips.

And then he felt it. Resistance against his hand. A small answering thrust. Tiny, but unmistakable. And another one. She used her thigh muscles to lift herself just a fraction and glide deeper along his length, giving a tiny twist of her hips at the bottom. Again, and again. Blood roared through his ears, need clawing desperately at his spine. She was taking what she wanted. In front of the sound tech. Taking Cassis on full display.

Now her eyes glowed with more than lust—they glowed with the same triumph he'd just felt himself. Her body fit so perfectly against his that Cassis risked losing himself with each of her small movements.

"What would you like me to do about the sound, sir?" Leroy prompted, shifting his weight with unusual impatience. His voice seemed to be coming from a thousand miles away now, through a tunnel of fog. Though the male kept his head down, Cassis could see the hard bulge growing inside the tech's trousers. And to his own surprise—and dismay—he didn't like it one bit. Usually, he was "the more participants the better" when it came to sex.

"Nothing. Leave it as is," Cassis barked at the male, sparks of red suddenly flickering at the sides of his vision. Damn it. What the hell was happening to him? How was he losing at his own game? "Leave us as well."

It was all Cassis could do to keep from swinging at Leroy, the male's speedy retreat not feeling quick enough.

"He's gone," Cassis whispered into the witch's ear, bracing himself as her victorious self-control buckled. Her back arched, her hips bucking to move along Cassis's shaft. His own cock demanded the same damn thing. For just a moment, they let their bodies take over, fucking openly, grinding against each other with desperate, if restrained, hunger. The bench creaked rhythmically under the loud music, the wet slap of their bodies sounding somewhere farther below that, and Cassis couldn't bring himself to care. He touched her clit again, felt the swollen need, the gaping abyss that awaited them both. So close. So agonizingly far away.

For a moment, Cassis considered bringing the witch upstairs and finishing this in style. His shower—and bedroom, and every other surface in his apartment—was certainly no stranger to various types of *finishes.*

Except it was different with Samantha. Real. And he wasn't ready for real. Not yet. Maybe not ever. Judging from what had happened to Ellis and Reese the moment they completed the mating act, the bond between them and Sam snapped into place. Which left Cassis only one choice here.

But he'd give her what she craved first.

He licked his fangs, the essence of Sam's blood still clinging to the sharp enamel from when he'd grazed her thigh. Her magic had bubbled through her blood like fine champagne effervescence, her arousal giving it a thick taste that would haunt Cassis for eternity. One tiny lap, and the witch had ruined his desire for entertainment with anyone else. Though maybe she'd done it long before tonight.

His head and cock pulsing, Cassis focused all his attention on Sam's sex, grazing the hot nub with the rough pad of his thumb. The spasm of orgasm raked through her small body in stunning waves, and she bit hard into his shoulder to keep from screaming through the club. He closed his eyes against her beauty, pain ratcheting through him as he held back his own release. He held her waist tighter, feeling how the lack of ability to move fed her arousal. How another well-placed thrust drove her to a second orgasm, her muffled sounds vibrating against his chest. How her satisfied body sank limp into his, every ounce of her weight held up by him alone. How his cock was still stone hard in her velvety warmth.

He stroked her hair, his heart tightening at the feel of her resting against him. Once her breathing evened out, Cassis lifted Sam off his erection and packed himself with difficulty back into his pants. If she noticed that he hadn't finished inside her, she was too exhausted to question it. And he planned to keep it that way.

FIVE MINUTES LATER, Cassis leaned his forehead against the shower tile, his release still shuddering through him as he let the cold, cold water grip his body. After the luscious heat of Sam's body, his own hand was almost comically disappointing. But it had to be this way. He wasn't ready to take a female, and given what finishing inside Sam would likely mean, he had to do whatever necessary to keep his libido in check around her. A nearly impossible task with that sweet citrusy smell still rocketing through his senses, even though she was all the way downstairs—and still without underwear. Bloody hell. One thought of the witch's missing underwear, and all the effort he'd put into getting himself together was tossed out the window.

Sighing, he turned the neck of the wolf-shaped faucet to shut off the water and toweled himself off. Painful cock or not, they still had Asher and the little urchin to deal with, and neither problem was going to take care of itself.

Slipping into a fresh set of slacks and French-cuffed shirt, Cassis hesitated a moment in front of his dresser. Destroyed panties were a common enough casualty of passion that Cassius had a few new sets tucked away for emergencies. The question was how Samantha might react if he showed up with a pair of thongs to offer.

Not well, most likely.

Regardless, he needed to go downstairs—Asher was due any minute. and he wouldn't leave Samantha to face the fae bastard alone.

1 6

———

ASHER

*A*sher strode into Dusk, putting a hand up to guard his eyes against the pulsing lights that demanded his attention from all sides of the bar. Flat screens intermittently zoomed in on the strippers decorating several pedestals and zoomed out to give a filtered overview of the dance floor, where a variety of gorgeous creatures—mostly vamps—were enjoying themselves to the fullest. Asher paused a moment, waiting for that instinctive spark of arousal that an abundance of females should spark in a wolf.

Nothing.

Ironically, the only female his body seemed interested in nowadays was the one he not only couldn't have, but also wanted nothing to do with. He took a steadying breath. At least there were no Talonswood cadets amidst Dusk's patrons tonight. The last time Asher had been here, with Reese, there'd been juveniles doing shots at the bar.

Catching sight of Cassis at a booth near that bar, his hand sprawled over the back of the bench seat, Asher headed toward the vamp. The text asking Asher to meet him here was the first of its kind the male had sent, well, ever. The last time Asher and Cassis were on any kind communication basis, cell phones had not yet been invented.

Coming close to the booth, Asher realized the vamp wasn't alone. Rather, he sat beside a female, his fingers casually winding around a lock of red-streaked hair. Asher's stomach clenched. Surely the witch would not have been so stupid as to come to Dusk *and* allow Cassis to summon him here. No, of course not. It had to be another female.

Yet that possessive, primal set to the vamp's eyes was something Asher had only ever seen when Samantha was around.

A few more steps and he'd have his answer.

"Asher," Cassis said lazily, the vamp's British accent making the r nearly disappear.

Sitting beside him, Samantha—yes, God damn it, it was her—stiffened. Anxious, but unsurprised. She'd known he was coming. Unable to stop himself, Asher focused his entire being on the witch, on the smooth thighs under that pert little uniform skirt, her breasts pressing against a slightly rumpled white-collared shirt. Her high cheekbones, flushed with tension —or was it something else causing that delicate pink blush to crawl up her smooth skin? His nostrils flared suddenly as he took in the lingering musk of arousal on her skin. Then a second, spicy male scent. The same one coming from Cassis. Fuck.

They'd coupled. Or had come damn close to it. It shouldn't matter. It didn't matter. What mattered was that the witch had violated Asher's orders and needed to be taught obedience.

"Cassis," Asher said, giving the vamp a cool half bow before locking eyes with the witch. "Samantha. You've made an interesting choice coming here tonight."

Her spine straightened. "Yes. I did."

"I hope you still feel that way when we return to campus."

Cassis's hand froze its motion. Bracing his forearms on the table, the vampire leaned toward Asher. "That sounded too much like a threat for my taste," he said quietly, the promise of menace in his voice going deeper than Asher had heard in decades. His scent shifted too, becoming sharper. More primal and dangerous. Cassis didn't know about the new Academy rules, then, and—for reasons of her own—Samantha had chosen not to tell him. Cassis opened and closed his hand before taking a sip from the glass of whiskey before him. "If I were in your shoes, I'd worry more about yourself than the witch tonight."

Shifting the Samantha situation into a back part of his mind to be dealt with later, Asher slid into the seat opposite the pair and signaled the waitress to bring him the same drink Cassis had. "Why *am* I here tonight?"

"Well"—Cassis leaned back, the cocky persona he wore like a cloak these days slipping around him easily—"it has to do with your cock. And your decisions. But mostly your cock."

Funny. A muscle in Asher's jaw ticked.

Samantha shot Cassis an exasperated glare, but the vampire only looked back at her lazily. Shaking her head, the witch turned her attention back to Asher, studying him intensely, like an artist getting ready to pick up a brush. "Nine...no, probably ten years ago," she said after a moment. "Were you by chance in London?"

Asher frowned, glancing at the ceiling as he counted back the trips and years.

"It's a good thing we only need ten years back," said Cassis. "He'd have to remove his shoes otherwise to help keep count."

Asher ignored him, slipping the last piece of memory into

place. "Closer to ten. Reesand was between military stints. I believe he was just coming out of the British SAS. Or going into it. Either way, I met up with him in London for about two weeks. I've not been to London, or any other part of the UK, since. What does it matter?"

"We'll be getting to that shortly," said Cassis, a corner of his mouth twitching up. "First, though, what kind of recreation did you engage in while you were there? Bowling, picture shows, museums? What struck your fancy?"

Asher glared at the bastard, because obviously Cassis already knew the answer. Just as the vamp knew Asher to be more private than most fae when it came to carnal pleasures. Fine. But this was the last indulgence Asher was granting this interview. "If you're asking whether I hired any entertainment," Asher said, shooting a warning glare at Cassis, "the answer is yes. When did my cock become your business?"

"About four hours ago."

Enough. Asher rose. He'd made an error in judgment thinking that Cassis would only have summoned him for something important. Though perhaps in the vamp's mind, letting Asher know that he and the witch had shared a bed *was* important. "I'm done here. Samantha, it would behoove you to return to the Academy with me."

"The result of your hired entertainment is sleeping in my guest bedroom," Cassis said, all humor now gone from his voice. "That is why I called you and Samantha here."

Asher froze, the dull sound of the words vibrating though his body as he stared at Cassis. The vamp's words were all there, ricocheting inside Asher's head. All comprehensible. But somehow, their combined meaning was not. "The *Arabian Nights* women are in your bedchamber?" Asher said, the question sounding idiotic even to his own ears. Last he knew, *Arabian Nights* was run by a vamp, so if one of the human escorts there desired transport to Talonswood, she would be able to find it easily enough. But to suggest that any of them would actually come looking for a stray client from ten years ago? "I still don't see what any of this has to do with me. I didn't even use my real name when I went."

"True," Samantha agreed, and for some inexplicable reason, Asher felt heat rise to his cheeks. Hell take him. He was blushing like a schoolboy. Sam bit her full bottom lip as if to quell a smile, which didn't help matters. "Would you have used the name Dust, by chance?"

"Possibly." Asher's slowly quickening heartbeat now pounded in earnest against his ribs. Taking the drink he ordered from the waitress's tray, he held it without taking a sip. "Are you two telling me that a woman I spent a night with in London ten years ago tracked me down to Dusk?"

"No," said Samantha, though her quiet tone did nothing to ease the pit of anxiety growing in Asher's stomach. "The woman died nine years ago. The guest sleeping upstairs is her son, Jake. And your son, I presume."

The glass in Asher's hand shattered.

He stared at the mess of glass and whiskey, shaking his head. "No," he said, repeating the word again, louder. He'd used a condom. Everyone at *Arabian Nights* did. The place even supplied them. He'd used a goddamn condom. "No. Impossible."

"Let me go wake Impossible up for you, sir." Sliding out of her seat, Samantha headed toward Cassis's upstairs suite with the confidence of someone who'd been there recently. With that short plaid skirt, rolled up so it barely covered her backside, the witch drew the eye of every male in the room— though the gazes fled away as soon as they touched her. The patrons' deference to Cassis's claim.

Pulling his gaze away from Sam, Asher looked blankly at Cassis. "I do not have a son."

"I don't give a damn." All humor dissolved from the vamp's face. "Samantha, on the other hand, I do care there. I want my bartender back."

"I want this morning back. Things were a lot more straightforward then." Asher flagged down a waitress and cleaned up the mess on the table, finishing just as two pairs of shoes appeared on the staircase leading down from Cassis's suite. Sam's black ankle boots and a pair of worn white Adidas sneakers.

Asher's heart quickened, his palms so moist, he wiped them on his jeans. Step by slow sleepy step, the boy himself entered into view. Small. Fierce. With the same golden hair and tawny eyes that Asher saw every day when he looked into the mirror to shave. Worn blue jeans hung off his skinny waist, and a baggy black T-shirt with all four faces of Queen on it couldn't disguise the fact that he hadn't been eating nearly enough. Asher stared, unable to move or speak.

Catching sight of Asher, the boy stopped dead too, squeezing Samantha's hand. The witch said something into his ear before letting that damn fire-breathing dragon of hers hop into Jake's arms.

That finally spurred Asher free of his stupor. "Put that thing down before you hurt yourself," Asher ordered loud enough to be heard across the room. "It breathes fire."

"Not that I'm an expert," Cassis murmured behind him, "but that hardly seems like the most efficient means to win friends and influence street urchins."

Asher didn't care. He'd just laid eyes on the boy, and he wasn't going to watch the cub be turned to ashes. Getting to his feet, he met the boy halfway to the booth. "I said—"

"I'm little, I'm not deaf. I know what you said." Instead of putting the dragon down as ordered, Jake held the animal closer to his chest as if it were an overgrown puppy. "Sam says your name is Asher. You look like me."

"It is. And yes, you look like me too." Weighing his options with battlefield swiftness, Asher let the dragon issue be and crouched before the cub instead, meeting him at eye level. The boy held his ground, his small features stiff with stubbornness. This close, Asher could see the freckles scattered across his cheeks. Fear and protectiveness mixed together inside him, neither making sense given that he'd just met the child. And yet there they were. "So, you're Jake? You've come a long way to find me."

"I took a plane. I think." He scratched his foot against his standing leg. "I don't remember."

Asher nodded. "There's usually a sleeping agent administered on the flight to the island." Was that the right answer to give a child? It was the truth. "For security reasons."

"Is that why you never came to get me?" Jake demanded, sticking his chin out. "For security reasons?"

Asher flinched. Right. "I didn't know you existed, Jake," he said quietly. "But now that I do——"

"Because I found you." Giving the dragon a final squeeze, the boy returned him to Samantha's arms and stepped so close to Asher that barely a foot of space remained between them. Close enough to touch, if that was what Jake wanted. The boy's small hand twitched. "The reason you know I exist is because I found you."

"Yes. Yes, you did." Asher held himself very still, lest he scare the boy. "Now that——"

"I am nine years old," Jake said, interrupting Asher midsentence. "And I found you. You're a grownup. A fucking immortal grownup. And you couldn't find me. So you know what?" Jake pulled back his fist and landed a hook right onto Asher's cheekbone. "Go to *fucking hell, you son of a bitch!*"

The boy shook his hand, wincing only slightly at what would have broken a nondemi's hand. Oh yeah, this was Asher's son, all right.

And before Asher—or anyone else—could recover, Jake turned on his heels and raced out of Dusk.

1 7

SAM

*A*sher's face turns pale, his tawny eyes wide and—for the first time since I met the male—filled with terror. I've never seen him like this, have never seen any of the males like this, not even in the middle of combat. Asher, who commanded fleets, who holds an entire Academy of delinquent immortals under rein, seems to have finally met the one foe who brings him to his knees.

A nine-year-old boy.

The door behind Jake slams closed, and Asher flinches as if struck. For a moment, he keeps standing there, his hands opening and closing at his sides. Then he turns to me, his heart pounding so hard that I can see each beat twitch against the sensitive skin on his neck.

"Samantha," he whispers. "Help me. Please. Help Jake."

My chest tightens at the desperation in the male's voice. Never in my life had I imagined I would ever hear Asher plead with me. Never would have thought how much I *don't* like seeing him like this.

I turn to Cassis. "Jake needs a bit of breathing room. Do

115

you have someone who can dog him for a bit and make sure he isn't hurt?"

Cassis waves his phone. "Already done. The last thing I need is for the urchin to be offering his services to the competition, don't you think?"

"His services?" Asher asks.

Cassis hooks a chair with his foot and kicks it toward Asher. "You don't want to know right now," he says, signaling the waitress for drinks. "But I would love to be there when you have that conversation. Your cub seems to share both your wonderful personality and my opinion of you, by the way." Cassis's phone pings. "My males have him in sight. How long do you want them to let him run, Sam?"

"So long as it's safe, until he is ready to stop." I sit at the small table beside us, Asher mirroring my movements. "Jake's emotions are all over the place right now," I tell the male. "It will take time. If we can avoid having you corner him like prey, things will go smoother."

My throat aches as I try not to think about all those years that made me such an expert on small, frightened, abused children.

"I don't understand," Asher whispers, his gaze shifting between the door and Cassis's phone, that now shows a shared location of the pursuing vamp team. "How is it possible that I have a son?"

"Ask Ellis. I'm sure he'd be more than happy to explain to you how pups are made," Cassis said, his voice edged with a vindictive satisfaction that fades before his next sentence. "Or, given the conversations we've had with Jake so far, the boy may be able to fill you in as well." He smiles at his phone. "And he's right back to Dusk, by the way. Out in back."

I grip Asher's forearm, the muscles beneath my fingers coiled tightly. "Shift into wolf form before going out there. It will be easier if he doesn't have to talk to you. Just stay beside him. As long as it takes. Let him choose to come to you."

Asher nods quickly, acknowledging the order without question or hesitation. A courtesy I'm certain I've never extended to him. Not really.

The air around him starts to shimmer.

"Belay that," Cassis says suddenly, though nothing about his face changes. "We have company that does not need to know about Jake's existence."

Asher halts his shift, solid fae once more as he takes his seat just in time to greet a tall, dark-haired vampire striding up to our table.

Victor. My stomach sinks.

"Good evening, Gentlemen. *Lady.*" The smooth Romanian accent hits the middle of my chest with sniper precision as the count stops next to us. It's bad enough that Asher's seen me out; I have no idea what Victor will do in retaliation. Especially now that his precious reputation—maybe even his job—is on the line with the council.

A heavy hand settles on my shoulder, and Cassis pulls me close to him in a gesture that's more primal than polite. Asher gets to his feet in a proper greeting to a superior officer, his body and face schooled to stone.

"Count Victor." Cassis crosses his legs. "If I knew to expect you today, I would have prepared more appropriately. Where is the rest of your entourage, if I might inquire?"

"At the Academy," Victor says easily, a hint of a smile that doesn't reach his eyes playing across his pale face before his attention drops to adjusting a blood-red ruby cuff link. "Asher brought it to my attention that perceived equality between cadets is a critical factor in discipline, safety, and the very core of the Academy mission. In deference to his insistence that, regardless of circumstance, every creature be subject to the same privileges and discipline, I no longer allow any cadets to accompany me off campus. Isn't that right, Commander?"

I can't help the shiver that runs down my spine.

Asher's schooled features never waver as he takes his seat again. "It is, sir," he says off-handedly. "Will you be joining us this evening?"

"I'm afraid this isn't a social visit, but rather a conversation I need to have with Dusk's proprietor. It's only polite to leave the choice of the venue up to him."

Cassis accepts the ordered drinks from the waitress and takes a slow sip before eying Victor up and down. My pulse quickens. I'm no vamp, but even I know a pissing contest when I see one. "What can I do for you, Count?" Cassis finally asks.

Reaching into his pocket, Victor takes out several photographs of a small passenger plane, laying them on the table. "This craft landed on one of my bases in Romania. I fear the tail number is unregistered, but I thought the visual might jog your memory. I have the specs here as well. If this plane is by chance yours, I would be happy to make arrangements to have it returned."

Flipping through the pictures with his free hand, Cassis shakes his head dismissively. "It doesn't look familiar in the least. You may wish to check with your own companies. The craft looks small enough that its absence might not have risen to your attention."

Victor's dark eyes flash with ice, but he simply gathers the pictures and tucks them away. "Of course. Do not let me interrupt your evening any further, then. I imagine I will see at least two of you back on Academy grounds in the morning?" The last is plainly rhetorical, and Victor doesn't wait for an answer, striding out through a parting sea of nodding, half-bowing vamps.

Asher's stony mask falls the moment the door closes behind Victor, his tawny gaze heavy. "Samantha—"

I shake my head quickly, not wanting him to continue. Victor knows I'm here, which ties Asher's hands when it comes to discipline. That's the risk I took when I decided to answer a friend's call for help, and when I stayed to help a young boy. Whatever Asher or Victor decides to do now, I wouldn't have done it any differently. "Jake is waiting for you. Go."

The air around Asher shimmers, and a white wolf with golden highlights takes the male's place, padding softly out toward the back door. I watch him go, waiting a few extra heartbeats before returning my attention to Cassis. "What was that about?"

The vamp's nostrils flare. "Victor has my plane," he says with quiet fury. "But it's been emptied."

I swallow. "What was it carrying."

"Not what," Cassis corrects. "Who. Two dozen donors."

"I don't understand."

Cassis sighs and shoots me a look that says *don't be so naïve.* "Where do you think all this blood you serve at yonder bar comes from, Samantha? Do you imagine I kill people on a regular basis?"

I do my best not to cringe. "It doesn't come from blood banks?"

"Like what, the Red fucking Cross? I would no sooner serve something after they've treated it than you'd drink from a chlorinated pool. I employ human donors directly. Keeping them safe is my responsibility."

"But your plane went missing." I watch Cassis's face as a rare moment of raw concern paints his beautiful features. His throat bobs, a shadow of pain brushing his dark gaze. These people he brought over, he cares about them. A lot. "So do you think Victor kidnapped the passengers?" I whisper. "Was that a ransom demand just now?"

"No. It was a message. I think the bastard is actually trying to help me—enemy of my enemy is my friend and all that." Cassis's hand tightens around the edge of the table, his already pale knuckles going bone white. "Talonswood usually has a steady flow of mortals coming in and out for various jobs, but things have shifted. Now, whole planeloads land without anyone available for employment. The word on the darker streets is that a certain fae syndicate is rounding up humans and forcing them through the gateway on a one-way trip to Talon. As I make it a point to stay the hell out of other creatures' business, I've responded to this by taking extra precautions with my deliveries. A *keep your bloody hands off* stamp, if you will. Until two days ago, that's been enough." Closing his eyes, Cassis takes a long drink. "Things have changed."

My mouth dries. "Are you saying *Bryant* is running a slave operation? It goes all the way to the top?"

"Of course he is. Well, at least his minions are." Cassis twirls his glass, watching the whiskey going in twisting circles. "And now that I know they have people under my protection, I'm going to have to do something about it."

18

ASHER

"I hope last night treated you well?" Count Victor said, walking beside Asher as he dismissed the cadets off the green following the completion of their morning detail. It was the second morning of liberty Asher had robbed them of in the name of cooperating against a common enemy—him. And a beautiful morning at that. A cool fall day, sun beaming over the campus, just the hint of crispness in the air. All over the green, trees were turning brilliant shades of orange and yellow. He could feel the resentment pouring off the cadets in waves as the morning grew late. If the week went well, he intended loosening the reins the following weekend.

At least that was the plan. After last night, Asher's mind and soul were a jumbled mess.

Samantha had been right about Asher's wolf form being more acceptable to Jake than his fae state. After initially running off, the boy had returned to the alley behind Dusk and settled under a bench for shelter. That was where Asher had spent the night as well, curled up as a wolf a few feet away from Jake, ready to rouse at the slightest bit of movement.

When he'd shifted in the morning to try to talk to the pup, however, Jake had run again.

This time, Asher gave chase. Manhandled him to the ground. Held him in place until Jake had finally kicked and cursed himself to exhaustion. Asher was about to congratulate himself on the victory when he realized that Jake had simply shifted tactics, refusing to acknowledge his presence. Holy hell. If all children were anything like Jake, it was a wonder anyone survived to adulthood.

They'd ended up settling the impasse by Asher calling Ellis, who had taken up residence not far from Dusk. That was where Jake was now. Where Asher should be too.

"Last night?" Asher echoed the vampire's question. Last night had taken Asher's world, turned it inside out while it was still alive, and then set it dancing on an internal flame. "It was unremarkable. Beyond finding Samantha at Dusk, of course."

Asher had no idea how long he could keep the boy a secret, but his gut told him he should.

"Of course," Victor agreed easily, his gaze following a group of demivamps with Christian at the lead, walking companionably beside Sam and Mika. Too companionably. Asher hid a frown. While this was the intent of his friendship-through-misery approach, seeing Christian beside Samantha was a little *too* convenient. Had Victor ordered the vampire students to befriend the witch? Victor laced his hands behind his back, the streaming sunlight casting harsh shadows across his angular features. "When will you be disciplining her?"

There was an undertone of glee in Victor's voice, buried so deep that Asher would have missed it if he hadn't been paying attention. Either Victor liked the idea of the witch being hurt in general, or—more likely—he liked that Asher specifically would be doing the hurting. It made for a clean *"vampires are nice and fae are cruel"* narrative. Not to mention that Victor no doubt sensed Asher's complicated feelings for Samantha. If he hadn't, he wouldn't have told Asher to keep his hands off her as part of their deal. This way, Victor would get to uphold discipline and hurt Asher in the process. A win-win of epic proportions.

"I am expecting her in my study in twenty minutes. It's hardly a complicated matter." The lie came easily.

"Very good." Victor gave him one of his signature half bows. "I will be nearby in case you require anything. Witches can be unpredictable creatures."

PACING along the window of his study, Asher had to admit that this was the first time in his life he was probably more anxious about a coming punishment than the cadet was. Because Samantha didn't know what she was facing, not really. And after what she'd done for him last night, she deserved better than what Asher was about to do to her. It made him feel somewhat better knowing that Sam had had no idea about Jake when she first left the Academy yesterday—but not by much.

Grabbing the leather lash from its hook inside a cupboard door, Asher rolled up his sleeve and tested the lash against the inside of his forearm, where the skin was more sensitive. More like a mortal witch's than a fae's. A blaze of pain shot across the raised welt, echoing to his elbow and fingers, but at least there was no immediate blood. Still, he was an immortal. Samantha was not. Mortal physiology wasn't something they'd accounted for when laying down the rules at Talonswood.

Victor probably made that calculation early on, when he was so insistent that Asher show no leniency to Sam. And now he was close by to ensure Asher didn't go astray. There wasn't a way out of this. Nothing changed the facts.

Asher sat down. Stood. Paced along the window.

A knock sounded. It was time.

Tossing the leather lash onto his desk, he rolled his shirtsleeve back down before opening the door to let the witch in. In her uniform of blue plaid skirt, blazer, and white blouse, she looked like any other cadet sent here, down to the familiar tang of anxiety lining her scent. But that was where the similarity ended. Her fire-filled hazel gaze burned right into Asher's soul, rousing too many emotions there. Her sweet citrusy scent had shifted from Dusk, no longer holding the traces of arousal and Cassis's musk.

Which shouldn't matter. Certainly should not rouse the hot streaks of jealousy in his gut. Send his blood coursing too quickly through his veins. So quickly that the star-shaped mark Sienna had carved into his left arm tingled and woke at Sam's presence. That was new. Asher had never felt the scar long for something before.

He nodded his greeting. At least she hadn't brought the dragon with her. The last thing they needed to add to the afternoon was a distraught reptile burning down a building. "Sit," he ordered.

Sam's eyes surveyed the room, lingering on the desk behind him, where he'd tossed the whip. Her shoulders tightened. "I prefer to stand."

The note of defiance in her voice pinged against Asher's already complicated instincts. The same went for how she positioned herself in the room, keeping a piece of furniture between them. Half of him was proud of the witch's spine, of not accepting anything without a fight. The other half of him, the predator half, was waking to the instinct she was baiting. To hunt. To conquer. To possess.

He stepped toward her.

She stepped back.

Fuck. Could the girl not stay still? His heart—and scar—pounded with a sudden primal need for her.

One that couldn't be indulged.

"We should get this over with," he said, proud of his calm, steady voice.

"You still intend to deliver a beating?" Sam asked him.

"Yes."

She shook her head, disdain spilling into her scent. "I thought yesterday changed something. Plainly, I was wrong."

"My life changed yesterday," Asher said, his tone low. Honest. "The rules of Talonswood Reform did not." He drew a breath. "You are getting six cuts, Samantha. I would rather they come from me than someone else."

"Of course you would." She swallowed, her hands trembling slightly despite a raised chin. "Seeing Jake yesterday, it reminded me of something. That I've met you before ever coming to Talonswood. Not *you* personally, but people like you. Ones more concerned about flexing their might than about anything else around them."

"That is not what this is about." Asher didn't know why he wanted her to believe him so badly, but he did. "I do not enjoy hurting you. Or any of the others. But I do what is needed to enforce that rule of law." He paused before the final order, then gave it. "Bare your back."

Samantha shrugged out of her blazer with her back to him, hanging it too neatly on the back of a chair, her blouse following suit. The long, smooth lines of her back, the creamy skin he was about to welt, made his throat clench. She reached behind to unhook her bra, hesitating for a moment with her fingers brushing the pale pink clasps. "Did you know that a syndicate of fae criminals is rounding up humans to send to Talon as slaves?"

Asher blinked, the answer spilling out before he could reconsider speaking at all. "No."

"No?" Sam unhooked the bra, the flimsy scrap of silk falling to the floor.

Asher silently cursed himself. His pulse pounded in his temples now, so fast he worried he'd black out. What the bloody fuck had he been thinking? He should have told her to keep her bra on—hell, he should have told her to keep her blouse on, its scant protection the least he could have offered a mortal. Plus, then he wouldn't be *here*, his hungry gaze brushing the swell of her breast as she turned, the dusky nipple growing taut in the cool air.

The last time he'd seen this much of Samantha's skin, it'd been her first night, when the sight of water running down her delicious, shivering body and her furious hazel gaze were just small hurdles to overcome. Then, she had just been a cadet—a beautiful cadet, yes, but a cadet nonetheless. Now, with Sienna's hundreds-year-old magic awakening, growing stronger every day, his scar pulsing, every fiber in his body orienting itself toward her, it was another thing entirely.

Oblivious to his spinning thoughts, Sam bent down to pick up the fallen garment and hesitated a moment before lifting her chin high and walking to put that away as well. "The island is barely the size of New York State, and you don't know mortals are being hunted and forced through a gateway about twenty minutes down the road?"

"I am aware that snatching is one of the many criminal activities that happen, Samantha," Asher snapped. "I do not condone it. I do not investigate it either, given that I have a different job. Is there a point to you bringing it up now?"

"A morbid curiosity about your priorities, sir. Nothing more."

"My priorities lie strictly with Talonswood Reform." Sliding the leather lash from his work table, Asher tapped it against his leg, his forearm still throbbing from the sting. "Six cuts. Put your palms on the wall."

19

SAM

I spread my palms on the wall, the wooden paneling smooth and cool beneath my fingers. I'm anxious. But I'm not scared like I can tell Asher wants me to be. This isn't my first thrashing, though the bastards in the foster system didn't bother with formality before bashing my head into the wall.

There was an hour there last night when I thought I saw someone different behind Asher's rigid facade. A male who cared, whose soul was raw over a little boy. But with the turn of the day, that male has disappeared. There was no sign of him at formation today, in his orders splitting the cadets into work details. The male I saw last night was a blip on a radar. An artifact. The real Asher is the one standing behind me, and he is the same asshole as he always was—a gorgeous, powerful asshole whose world revolves around beating underlings into submission, be it with a lash to a back or a magnet slid over a hard drive.

He is the same as all the others I've met in my life. None of them ever broke me. Asher won't either.

Feet shift behind me.

My shoulders tense, bracing for pain, my heart and breath both speeding.

And then they aren't.

I feel the force of the impact knocking me into the wall before the pain itself registers, a white-hot blaze that takes all my breath. Holy fucking hell. I'm dizzy for a heartbeat, my shield of self-certainty cracking down the middle.

A moment later, the pain comes again. My knees buckle, my nails digging into the wood as the world blinks around me. This is worse than anything I faced as a child. Asher's immortal strength makes it worse. I pant and brace myself as much as I can, as the magic inside me suddenly rouses, buzzing like a hive of bees in my blood.

Except this time, instead of making me stronger, my magic-enhanced senses make everything a thousand times worse. I hear the whistle of leather slicing air. Feel my skin splitting for the third time. Smell the leaking blood. The scar on my palm feels as though knives are driving into my flesh.

I scream, the sound echoing from the walls. My back feels like Asher has poured gasoline over my skin and struck a match. Nothing, *nothing* will let me escape the agony. Suddenly, I'm no longer in Asher's study, but in a dungeon cell, my hands strapped by iron manacles.

Agony rakes my body as I struggle helplessly against the iron binds Sienna clamped on me for punishment. My heart races so quickly, that it's a wonder it hasn't yet ripped itself apart. The smell of burned flesh fills my nose, coating everything in a thick mist of fear and darkness.

"Samantha!" A deep male voice reaches toward me through the void. "Draw some air."

I obey and choke immediately, the air pouring into my burning lungs making the pain worse.

A hand grips my shoulder.

I throw myself sideways to escape capture, only to slam into a solid male chest. A fresh sandalwood musk fills my nose, fingers digging into my upper arms while my back burns.

"Stay with me, Samantha," the familiar male voice demands, a pair of penetrating tawny eyes filling my vision.

"I…" I blink, gripping onto the familiar gaze like a lifeline. Asher. I can smell his fresh shampoo, the scent washing away the phantoms of old blood and mold and rust. Whose memory had I been in? Ellis's or Reese's? I swallow, remembering the iron. Ellis's, then. Not that it matters. The dungeon is gone, the manacles nonexistent. And as for me, I'm half naked in Asher's grip. And I hurt. I hurt so, so badly.

"I can't do this," I whisper, releasing all caution to lean into the male. I've never begged for reprieve in my life. But I can't take this. Can't endure more of the magic-enhanced pain that threatens to consume me, to send me right back to that holding cell from Ellis's memories.

"Asher." I appeal to the male I saw yesterday in Dusk, the male Ellis told me would do right by me when it counted. I rip through twenty years of distrust, of knowing that admitting weakness leads to being stepped on harder. I draw a shaking breath and let the tears welling in my eyes spill onto my cheeks. "No more. Please stop. Please."

Asher's tawny gaze glistens as it meets mine, his hands steady on my shoulders. "I can't stop," he whispers to me, the back of his hand wiping my face. "Victor saw you last night. There is no way in hell and beyond you're ending the day with fewer than six. The best—the *only* thing—I can do is ensure they come from me."

I stare at him dully, unable to fully listen as Asher continues to speak. It's something about the number three, and keeping clear of kidneys and some kind of platitude that all translate into a single word. The only one that matters, the one that hurts so much more than the lashing.

No.

I'd begged him for reprieve, and he said no.

As the full force and finality of that realization hits me, the weakness inside me snaps closed. Magic roars into its place, pouring into my muscles. Ready to battle. To run. But I know I can't. The only thing I can do is never ever again give Asher the satisfaction of seeing me beg, no matter how many shreds he tears me into.

Asher is still talking as I turn back to the wall, bracing my palm on the surface. I'm not listening. And I'm never straying from my instincts again.

2 0

SAM

I pause outside the dungeon entrance, a thick metal gate set deep into an ivy-covered stone wall, taking gulps of fresh air before going inside. The beautiful blue-sky fall day is an absurdity around me. The cadets bustle across the green. My back screams with every breath, but the pain is easier now that I'm out of Asher's presence. It's just mortal agony now, not a magic-born one. The lesson Asher seared into my flesh, however, that's still there loud and clear.

Maybe I should thank the male for the sharp reminder of reality. For helping me remember the perspective I've somehow lost. Don't trust anyone. Most especially men in power.

"Samantha."

Victor's polished voice makes me jerk in surprise, and I can't help cringing as I turn my face toward him. As usual, the count's slicked-back hair and perfectly tailored business suit make him look out of place among these solemn medieval stone buildings, like a Maserati in a covered-wagon caravan. He's the last person I expected to run into at this out-of-the-way corner of campus. And—with the notable exception of Asher—the last person I want to see just now.

"Sir?" I hug my balled-up blazer against my chest, since putting it on over my blouse was more pressure than I could bear in Asher's office. I might be able to put it on now, but it wouldn't do much good for my dignity at this point.

"I came to check how you were holding up." Victor's pale, aquiline features curve into a smile that manages to be sympathetic and condescending at the same time. He sighs. "For what it's worth, I attempted to talk Commander Asher into reducing the discipline. Physical punishment is the traditional penalty among fae and vampires, but witches have always been different. It's a matter of physiology really—what is but a temporary inconvenience for us is a graver experience to someone without immortal blood. Unfortunately, the Commander is highly…literal when it comes to regulations. It is what makes him a valuable officer most of the time, but certain situations call for more flexibility. Flexibility isn't Commander Asher's strong suit."

No shit, you noticed that too?

I bow stiffly and reach for the door, longing for the comfort of my cot and my dragon.

"One moment." Victor clears his throat. "I apologize for imposing when you're feeling unwell, but the other matter I wished to discuss is somewhat time sensitive. Well, it's sensitive all around. Tell me, when you were at Dusk with Cassis yesterday, did he mention anything about humans going missing?"

I brace my hand on the stone wall, squinting against the sun to buy myself time to think. The plane. Victor showed Cassis the photo of the plane, and my friend denied owning it. No sense denying the general concept, though, so long as I stay away from Cassis's blood-donor humans. "I know there are criminals who force humans through the gateway to Talon." I shift my weight, unable to hide a wince.

"Here." Reaching inside his jacket, Victor extracts and extends to me a small leather-bound flask. "You look like you need it."

I don't know what it is with vampires and alcohol, but at the moment, I'll take it. Twisting off the cap, I take a sip of the dark liquid, the strong bitter undertones mixed with something sweet. "What is it, sir?"

"Laudanum. A natural pain remedy." Victor drums a long finger impatiently against his wrist. "And did he mention that the disappearance rate has quadrupled in the last two months?"

"No, sir. With due respect, Cassis is a vamp—why would he have anything to do with taking humans to the fae realm?"

"He wouldn't," Victor says with surprising straightforwardness. "But since you trust the male, I was hoping you'd already heard the information from him. It would simply have made it easier for me to explain the situation."

"The situation, sir?" The sip of laudanum courses through me, taking the edge off the pain so quickly that I'm tempted to take another swallow, but decide against it.

"Snatching is getting out of control, despite all the council's attempts to put a stop to it. It's a moral offense against the humans as much as a practical danger for creature discovery. It must be stopped." Victor sighs. "And I'm afraid you may be the only one capable of doing so, Samantha. Before they bring in another batch of slaves two days from now."

I blink at him. "I'm sorry, sir, did you just say—"

"I did." He gestures to a worn low bench built into the side of the building, overhung with a dense honeysuckle bush. "Let's sit."

Yes. Let's.

I do take another sip from the flask at that statement, then hand it back with my thanks and stare at the count, wondering which one of us has gone utterly mad.

"Here in the mortal world, we live under rule of law, subject to the governance of the council of creatures. You know this." Victor pauses long enough for me to nod. "The council's jurisdiction ends at the Talon gateway, however. On the other side, Bryant rules with no one to answer to—and it's cost thousands of humans their lives. Unless you stop it, it will cost thousands more."

"What exactly do you imagine I can do, sir?" I ask.

He catches my eyes, his dark gaze utterly serious. "Close the gateway."

A shiver runs through me. "Close it? Like, permanently?" Except for a field trip driving all around the gateway building, I've never even seen the gateway portal, don't know what it looks like, what it's made of, how it works.

"Yes," Victor says softly, seeming to read my mind. "It's less complicated than it sounds, Samantha. The gateway is merely a passage like this one here"—he gestures to the arched opening leading down into the pitch-black of the dungeons —"but instead of a physical door on it, there's a magical one. And it closes with the same spell as everything else does. Just an extension of the closing spell you practiced on the locks."

I hear his words, but the sentences take a long time to compute. "Just a magical door."

"Exactly. It's about the size of a normal door too, though it shimmers rather than swings. Anyone can walk through it, though any trapping of the modern world they bring along won't work on the other side."

Victor sounds so conversational that for a moment, I forgot *why* he is telling me all this. Now, the reason returns. "But—me?"

"Magic created it, and only magic can close it. Which means if you do this, Bryant will be unable to open it again without a witch's help." He looks at me steadily, waiting for me to catch up.

I'm silent, not sure of my answer, let alone which questions to ask to arrive at one. I don't understand enough about this world yet to know all the ripple effects of such an action. Ellis's face rises into my mind. He's fae. What if he wants to go home? What if there are good fae—and I know there *are* other good fae besides my male—trapped in Talon who want to escape Bryant's rule?

A corner of Victor's mouth tugs sympathetically. "I realize it is a lot to take in, and I wish we had more time—but after seeing you call down the elements to dispatch an entire pack of fae warriors, I fear Bryant has come to the same conclusion I have. You are now powerful enough to close the portal. That means two things from his perspective: he needs to neutralize you if possible, and at the same time, he needs to take full advantage of the gateway while it's still functioning."

"Hence another batch of slaves."

Victor sighs. "Yes. Hence another batch of slaves." He straightens his long legs out before him, crossing the ankles. "With your magic, you can put a stop to it, Samantha. Let the fae have their own realm and lives as they choose, while letting the humans in this world live their own."

"What would happen to the Academy?" I ask, though I'm not really considering this. I can't be. It's too...too everything. "The demis. Everyone here?"

"Very little would change on this front," Victor says easily. "Talonswood Reform would operate as it always has, under council law. The fae who choose to live in the mortal world would continue to live their lives as they always have. The only difference would be a new lack of immunity for atrocities—no more access to an unreachable place for criminals to run to after committing mass murder."

I lean back, my back twinging in pain.

"You have met King Bryant, Samantha. Did he tell you the truth when you met? Do you doubt for a moment that he was behind the fae attack that killed and maimed so many of your classmates?" Victor pauses, the trill of sparrows in a nearby tree filling his silence. "Look beyond *my* words, Sam. Look at Ellis. I'm not fond of the male, but plainly, you are. Ellis is Bryant's son and has lived in Talon for centuries. But he's turned away from that realm now. As has Asher, who, if anything, is overly obsessed with the letter of the law. He turned his back on Talon hundreds of years ago. Two males who know the king better than anyone, who are as different from each other as brothers can be—they've both made the decision to separate themselves from Bryant's foulness. Look at their actions. See them for what they are."

Holy shit. The male is serious. I swallow, my body suddenly too hot for comfort. "Shouldn't...shouldn't something of this magnitude come from the council, sir?" I say, then wish I could take the words back. The last thing I can deal with right now is another irate male.

Victor appears to take no offense, however. "It should. But bureaucracy has never moved at the speed of life. Do you imagine the fae will want to cut off their highway to the place that shelters them from the law? Bryant has a seat on the council too—do you imagine for a second he'll willingly hand over power? Waiting for the council will mean waiting until you graduate and take your place there to represent the witches. If Bryant lets you live that long. If he hasn't already put defenses in place against exactly such a thing. You aren't here by chance, Samantha. You're here to fulfill a destiny. And it's time."

Victor leans closer to me, his body blocking out everything around me. His pupils dilate, becoming large and dark and all-consuming as a thick, warm blanket settles over my thoughts. "You are in danger from the fae, Samantha. They just discovered the extent of your power. They will try to destroy you. To fortify the gateway. You must close it. Tomorrow. With me. Tell no one. Thousands of innocent humans are depending on you."

ASHER

*A*sher leaned his forehead against the door Sam had just fled through, his body shaking. The events of the past quarter hour replayed themselves in his mind over and over again, an endless loop that took his breath. He'd been as unprepared as Sam at how overwhelming she'd found the pain. For some damn reason, he'd never expected to see tears. The witch never cried. But she had today. From the look of betrayal in her eyes, he'd hurt Sam deeper than the lash had touched, and that raked his soul. He didn't know how to make it better. If such a thing was even possible.

It wasn't supposed to be this way. Hell, nothing about the past two days was supposed to have gone the way it did.

Resisting the urge to rush out after Samantha, who clearly wanted to get as far as possible from him, Asher gave the clock a whole hour before allowing himself to head over to the infirmary. It was all he could do to keep his steps to a purposeful walk, instead of running like a berserk rabbit over campus. Once he was inside however, he set course directly for Reese's office.

"How is she?" Asher demanded, leaning a hand on the doorframe. The office was in perfect military order, the scent of antiseptic wafting in from the adjacent treatment room. "Is she all right?"

Reese kept his impassive blue eyes on his paperwork—notes from the day's sick-call visits, from what Asher could see over the vamp's large shoulder. "If you're asking about Samantha, I don't know. She didn't come here."

The utter lack of emotion in the vampire's tone struck Asher as much as Reese's words. "She must have come," Asher said dumbly, unable to keep his voice in check the way Reese had. "She was in bad shape."

"*Must* and *Samantha Devinee* rarely go together in one sentence," said Reese, his attention still on his fucking files.

"Damn it, Reesand. I'm telling you discipline went badly. Very badly. And if she isn't here, then—"

"Then I suggest you find her before I do." The pencil Reese held cracked in his hand. He lifted his head, his eyes flashing with leashed violence. "Better yet, if it was going badly, maybe you should have stopped."

Anger blazed through Asher's blood, heating his face. "And let Victor make it a hundred times worse for her when he discovered marks missing from her back?" He slammed his palm against the doorframe, which groaned beneath the impact. "Victor made the consequences of my *not* holding Samantha to iron standards crystal clear when he gave me control of the students. Don't fuck with me by pretending not to know that."

"Then I see no reason for your outburst." Each of Reese's words came in a low menace. "Seems to me that you got everything you wanted. Rules upheld. Culprit punished. A worse fate avoided. Isn't that what you are doing here at

Talonswood Reform? Preventing a *worse fate* yet from sweeping through the creature ranks?"

"Reese——"

"What more do you want?" Reese demanded. "This morning's formation was perfect. Victor quit favoring the vamps. Ellis and I both yielded to your decree to stay away from Samantha. The cadets have united, the infighting almost gone. Hades, it sounds like even the witch herself yielded to you just now. In fact, if the council came tomorrow, they'd find Talonswood in perfect order."

Asher flinched. Samantha *had* yielded, that spark of rebellion in her flickering out under his lash so expeditiously that it made bile rise up his throat. "Are you going to help me find her or not?" Asher pushed himself away from the door. "I thought you'd be coming at me with fangs bared to go offer comfort."

Reese's face darkened. "If I lay eyes on what you did to her, I *will* come at you with fangs bared," he said in a low voice. "It's unlikely both of us would survive that encounter. I recommend you find her and fix things before I do——and my patience with giving you a head start is wearing thin."

Right. Asher turned to leave.

"Commander Asher, pick up line two," the overhead intercom, a seldom-used antiquity in the age of smartphones, suddenly boomed through the building. "Commander Asher, line two please."

Without so much as looking at Reese, Asher grabbed the desk phone receiver. "Asher."

"This is security, sir. I'm in the kitchen area, and there's a child here who says his name is Jake. He——"

"I'm on my way." Asher felt a frustrated growl rumble through his chest as he slammed down the receiver. This wasn't the time. And why the hell hadn't Ellis told him he was bringing the boy here, much less let him run loose through the place? Turning on his heels, Asher strode out of the infirmary.

Flinging open the kitchen door, he walked past the stainless steel appliances and long metal prep table to the back of the room, where Raulle the cook and a guardsman, stood leaning over something. As Asher got closer, he saw Jake huddling on the floor below him. "What's going on?"

"The filthy urchin stole into my kitchen." Raulle spoke first, the words exploding from him as if they'd been bottled up for eternity. The male, a gigantic, swarthy vamp from France, wore a starched white apron and an apoplectic expression. "I was making the soup when this…child dashed in, wreaking havoc. He knocked over two pots and changed the temperature on the oven before I caught on to him. Ruined a batch of today's dinner. All burned. The meat is ready for the dumpster."

"I just wanted some bread," Jake shot back. Pressed into the corner, the boy stared out with defiant tawny eyes and wet cheeks. Ellis had somehow found him a new shirt overnight to replace that ratty Queen number—a clean blue-and-white-striped polo, probably from a very small first year. "Wasn't my fault that instead of just turning the dial back, he started chasing me around the kitchen."

Now that Asher looked closer, he could see Jake cradling his arm to his chest. Raulle had done more than just give chase. An irrational wave of rage pulsed through Asher, and he braced a hand on the wall just to get control of himself. How was it possible to feel so protective of a creature who, just a day ago, he didn't even know existed? Hell, how was it possible to want to embrace and strangle someone all at the same time?

"What did you do when you caught the boy?" Asher asked Raulle.

"Less than I should have," Raulle snapped before turning to Jake. "Less than Commander Asher is going to do to you."

Jake paled, cringing away. Like Samantha had. Fuck.

"What did you do to him?" Asher shouted, twisting toward Raulle, the room around him suddenly pulsing with his own heartbeat. "What did you do?"

"Nothing." Raulle rocked back on his heels, his huge hands up in a gesture of innocence. "I rapped his knuckles with a spoon. Surely this menace deserves—"

Asher didn't wait to hear Raulle's opinion of what Jake deserved. Crouching to the boy's level, he reached for the injured arm, bringing a small, swollen hand into the open. The skin was split on two of the knuckles, puffy skin in black, blue, and red hues stark again his pale complexion. The cub was so small and vulnerable under all his bravado. And hurt. Injured. Asher's heart hammered against his ribs, blood rising to his face.

"The child broke into my kitchen, destroyed property, and attempted to steal." The cook's voice rose with each indignant word, his French accent becoming more pronounced. "I demand he be disciplined immediately. We have rules here, Commander Asher."

"Everyone but Jake is dismissed," Asher snapped through a clenched jaw.

"This is my kit—"

"I said, get *out*." Asher spun to glare at Raulle and the wide-eyed guard who was still there, keeping his gaze on the males until their footsteps beat an even retreat along the tiled floor. Then he pulled out his phone. Two missed calls from Ellis flashed on the screen, along with the *silent mode* icon Asher had forgotten to change after Sam left his office. Below that, a single text message, also from Ellis.

Pick up your fucking phone. Jake wants to see you. Dropped him at Academy, since you won't let me in.

Damn it. Asher paused for a second, then dialed Reese. "I need you in the back kitchen," he said, shutting off the line before the vamp could ask questions. This wasn't a conversation to have over the phone. Scooping Jake into his arms—the boy was heartbreakingly light for a nine-year-old cub—Asher sat him on the edge of the prep table and raked his mind for some idea of what to say to him. To his *son.*

"I know how to lead armies," Asher said finally. "How to forge good soldiers and sailors. I have no idea how to raise a cub."

Jake recoiled.

Realizing the perceived rejection in his statement, Asher held up his hand and quickly amended himself. "What I mean is that this is something we will have to figure out together. Trust will take time, but can we at least agree not to purposely sabotage each other?"

"What does that mean?" Jake asked.

"It means, for starters, you do what I say."

Jake raised his chin. "What if I don't like what you say?"

Then you do it anyway. Asher caught himself before saying the words. "I don't know," he said instead. "But at the very least, you tell me. No more stealing, though. And no more running off."

"What about..." Jake's throat bobbed, his tawny gaze scurrying about the wrecked kitchen. "Are you going to punish me?"

"I'm going to give you the damn mess hall schedule so you can eat whenever you want." Asher turned to the sound of familiar footsteps as Reese's large frame filled the doorway. Fury and darkness still saturated the air around the vamp, but he'd come. Thank whatever deity was out there for that.

"What do you—" Reese cut off midsentence, the usually unflappable fighter staring dumbly as Asher stepped to the side to give him a clear view of Jake sitting on the kitchen table.

"Reesand, this is Jake. My son," said Asher, the word foreign and heavy on his lips. "Long story that started in London ten years ago and ended in Dusk. If you could hold off tearing me to pieces long enough to examine—"

That was as far as Asher got.

Jake scampered to the floor, putting the long table between him and the vamp. The boy's chest heaved with short rapid breaths, his heart beating so quickly, Asher could see it pulse on the side of his neck. The scents of fear and determination filled the air, the boy's glance at the window giving Asher the only warning he had of what was about to happen.

Reese was already moving, his speed and insurgent training cutting off the cub's escape route. Jake hesitated only a moment before aiming a foot at Reese's shin and making a valiant dodge around the male.

Snatching Jake around his waist, Reese deposited the still-kicking cub right back on the kitchen table.

Jake snarled.

Reese raised a patient black brow.

Asher stood like a bewildered fucking deer.

"Do you want to try those introductions again, Asher?" Reese said calmly, his gaze trained on Jake.

Introductions. Right. Asher hadn't even considered how the word *examine* might sound or how Reese's size and brooding aura might come across to an injured child. Probably not all that different from how he himself looked towering over Samantha when she pleaded for reprieve. Asher braced himself against the edge of the table, his throat tight. "Jake, my friend Reese is a medic. I wanted him to look at your hand."

Moving with a great deal more care than Asher had, Reese held out his palm and waited as long as it took for the child to volunteer the injured limb. The vampire had always had more patience. He should have been the father.

"Is it broken?" Asher asked, peering over the vamp's shoulder. He would disembowel Raulle, one slice for every fractured little bone.

"I highly doubt it," said Reese.

"You aren't sure?" Asher's pulse spiked again.

"Short of X-ray vision, no." Reese patted Jake's shoulder. "Think you can keep some ice on this while you eat with your other hand?"

"Ice?" Asher jerked around toward the vamp. "That's your solution?"

"No. My solution also involves dinner, which seems more important to the boy right now." Reese gripped Asher's gaze, the vampiric dominance he usually kept in check in deference to rank now taking hold. "It's a bruise, Asher. *He* will be fine. As for *you,* get a bloody grip on reality. If Jake is your son, he is half fae. He'd heal quickly even if the bones were broken. Stop fixing things that don't need fixing and deal with ones that do."

2 2

S A M

The soft sound of feet against stone jerks me upright. I've barely moved since burying myself in my cot, the combination of Victor's ambush and Asher's punishment echoing through me. The sudden blaze of pain along my back makes me regret doing so now. Especially when I see Asher.

In place of his usual uniform or training gear, the male wears blue jeans and a soft black sweater that look far too casual on his honed body. With his chiseled jaw and cropped blond hair showing off strong cheekbones, Asher looks more like a *GQ* model than a centuries-old battalion commander.

I swallow, my magic rising at the male's proximity. Given what the magic does to my senses—and pain receptors— waking it is the last thing I want just now. But Asher is about to demand, not ask, for my attention, and I've learned better than to casually defy the male.

He knocks on the stone outside my cell. It doesn't make much of a sound, but given that the bars don't make much of a wall, the knocking itself seems rather irrelevant. Seeming to have come to the same conclusion, the male lets himself inside, rousing Kitten from his nap at the foot of my bed.

For a moment, the male and I just stare at each other. He seems far too large for this space, his towering height and fresh male scent suddenly making it feel like a claustrophobic cubbyhole. "Reesand told me you never went to the infirmary," he says finally.

"I didn't know that was required, sir." I hate how much my stomach tightens, the way anxiety curls through me just at the possibility of a misstep. Maybe one day I'll have the courage to cross Asher again. But not today. Not tomorrow either. *Unless you decide to hop in bed with Victor and close the gateway.* "I can—"

"There is no requirement." Asher hesitates in the middle of the room, watching Kitten take flight and soar about the perimeter. The dragon has been feeling antsy since I returned, but I can't make myself go outside, or worse, let him tap into the magic he wants to drink.

Asher's attention slides back to me, the tawny gaze waking my body. I'm suddenly aware that I'm wearing no bra, only an oversized shirt over pajama pants—while Asher looks ready for a photo shoot. Worse yet, in the chill of the dungeon, my nipples have bunched into hard peaks that press against the fabric. Asher's gaze stays on my face. "I just meant that tending to the wounds can help take the edge off. I… I've been on both sides of the experience enough to know."

It's hard to imagine Asher in my place, except that I'm rather certain he'd never dissolved into a puddle of tears and begged for mercy.

"Yes, sir." I grunt as Kitten dives down and knocks himself against my chest, doubling me over. Pain washes over my back, the grunt morphing to a gasp as I wobble precariously.

I don't realize Asher has moved until his hands brace my shoulders, his earthy sandalwood scent wrapping tightly around me. "You're still bleeding," he whispers in surprise. His callused hand brushes the back of my neck, waking my skin to his touch. Up close, I realize his eyelashes are long and dark—much darker than his hair. Maybe that's what makes his golden-brown eyes so fucking riveting.

"Goddammit." The last comes under the male's breath, his grip on my shoulder tightening. "The punishment was never meant for a mortal."

I don't say anything. I hate how good it feels to have Asher's warmth beside me, to hear him utter those words, when his very presence makes fear course through me now. Everything inside screams to run, to get as far from this male as I can before collapsing, and yet my body refuses to move.

Turning me slightly, Asher raises the back of my shirt, the tips of his fingers gently brushing my bare shoulder. Cool air kisses my skin, and Asher swears quietly. Passionately. "I never intended for any cadet to be hurt this badly," he says. "And I know it *was* bad for you."

My heart pounds, though I can't tell whether it has more to do with my fury at the male's audacity to manhandle me like this, or with the impact that touch is having on my body. My bones feel soft, heat flooding through me, making my skin flush. My body's misguided attraction is a force of nature in itself, a colossal *fuck you* to my better reason.

Easing my shirt back into place, Asher pulls away enough to put his hand on my chin, tipping my face toward him. "There was no choice. Not by the time you were in my office. I couldn't stop even though I knew you hurt, and I sure as hell can't undo it now," Asher says into the crackling air between us, his earthy scent filling my nose. The contrast between his warmth and the cold, mildewy dungeon tingles over my skin. "But I want to help. If you let me."

I draw a shaking breath, letting Asher's words echo inside

me. And damn me, I do want to let him. I hurt and want to be cared for, want for someone to tell me that I will be all right. That he will make me all right. But that's what got me in trouble in the first place, wasn't it?—thinking that I could go toe to toe with this male and come out standing? That I could trust him?

I shake my head before my body can override reason. "Please let me go, sir."

He does. Immediately. Though his deep tawny eyes flash with pain. "Of course." He steps back, his long legs taking him halfway to the door in a second. "Reconsider seeing Reese, though. He might —" He cuts off with a frown. "Where did the dragon go?"

Confusion rolls over me as I turn about the room, not seeing the Kitten. He has to be here. The little beast can't turn invisible, as far as I know, and there's no place for the stinker to go. Then my eyes narrow on the grating beyond Asher's shoulder.

"You left the door open," I say.

"I…I don't like closed prison cells."

Well, good for you. I rush to the open grating, my aching body dropping to a distant second place in my consciousness. "Kitten!"

No response. Fuck.

Asher appears beside me in a second, the emergency flashlight from my wall gripped in his hand as he shines a bright beam over the stony landing. The corridor opening up around me looks as it always does, a dark, mossy, stone-lined passage on the right that disappears into the bowels of the dungeon, and a wider, better-lit walkway on the left that leads past the old guards' break room and bathroom to the stairs up to the entrance. "He probably wanted to go out," I say, turning left without bothering to pull on shoes. "Kitten!"

The male catches up to me quickly, blocking my path. "Stop," he orders, his gaze unfocused, his head tilted slightly. "I hear something in the other direction."

I close my eyes to listen, but my hearing has nothing on a fae's. Gritting my teeth, I reach inside me toward the coil of magic in hopes of getting a picture from Kitten. My senses waken, turning my back into an inferno that has me gasping for breath. "Damn it." I yank back as if from a scalding stove.

"What happened?" Asher asks, his voice thick with concern.

"I tried to tap into my magic to call him, but it amplifies," I say through gritted teeth. "I can't bear it just now."

Asher freezes, his gaze narrowing on me. "Doesn't your magic also bubble up when you're threatened?"

I blink. "Yes."

Blood drains from his face. "Say, because some bastard is taking a lash to your back? Would your magic amplify your senses then too?"

"It would," I say quietly.

Asher lets out a long slow breath before pulling himself back to task and shining his flashlight's bright beam down the dimly lit right corridor. "Your dragon went that way. I'm certain."

I nod, falling in step beside him as we start into the flickering darkness. Ten yards in, the worn, centuries-old floor starts sloping down at a steep angle, the already scant electrical wiring pared down to the occasional overhead lightbulb swinging on its own cord. The smell of underground dampness fills my nose, sending a shiver through me.

"How big is this place?" I ask to break the eerie quiet.

"It's large." Asher keeps his light moving from left to right, illuminating the stone walls with bits of moss growing along them. In the deepening dark, his tall, strong body towers over mine and his warmth brushes my skin, anchoring me to the here and now. I think about having to do this search alone and shudder. When I see fresh scorch marks on one corner, I know he's right about the direction of Kitten's excursion. Shit. I hate it here. The very air feels heavy, laden with oppression and misery.

"The room you're staying in used to be a general holding cell for large groups, like a crew of a captured vessel," Asher says, his voice low and calm. Soothing. "Officers would be separated into a smaller space, but historically treated with courtesy due their rank. It's the lower levels that house what most people think of as a dungeon, with cells for criminals and interrogation chambers."

Lower levels. Like the ones we're heading to now.

Asher touches my arm. His golden-brown eyes shine in the dimness, almost like they provide their own light. "Think of it like a museum," he says softly. "It helps."

I nod. Admittedly, it's oddly comforting to know that the chamber Asher put me and Kitten in did not host real torture. But I still hate it here. Viscerally.

I hear a rustling of wings in the distance and quicken the pace. "Kitten!" I call into the darkness.

No response. I don't know why I even expected one, given that the dragon has never responded to voice commands before. As we get closer, however, I feel a tickle along my magic, a sense of curiosity that is most certainly not mine rippling through my blood. Whatever the little stinker is doing, he finds it amusing.

"I think we're close," I tell Asher.

"Yes, I hear him." Asher's light illuminates the next turn in the passage. "It sounds like he's playing with metal rattles, of all things."

We turn the corner, and the room I never wanted to see

opens up beside us. Beyond the grating, manacles dangle from bolts on the wall, rusted wicked tools hanging in a horrific display of torment. In the middle of the sloping floor, just beneath the single lightbulb dangling on a frayed cord, is a kind of table with various joints and levers that makes me ill just from looking at them. And yet, there is also my Kitten, perched on an outcropping of rock as he alternately bats at a pair of clattering manacles and breathes fire to his heart's content. A playground. My dragon has found a torture chamber and turned it into a goddamned playground.

Drawing a breath of musty air, I find the light switch and breathe a word of thanks to electricity for still working and to the rusty door for not having clicked closed all the way behind Kitten and start into the cell. Behind me, Asher pushes a wooden wedge under the open grating to ensure it stays in place before following me inside, his breathing quicker than usual.

I look back at him and notice a faint gleam of sweat on his brow, feeling a stab of guilt. This is the last place he'd ever want to be—and yet he's here, keeping his fear to himself.

"Kitten." I try not to breathe in the dank air or look too long at the rusty drain in the corner of the sloping floor as I walk past the torture rack to the dragon's stony perch. The *clink clink clink* of the manacles he bats with his wing sound like an ominous metronome. "Kitten, let's go."

I hold my arm out to him.

Blinking at me with yellow eyes, the damn reptile takes flight right over my head, circling the whole place twice before wrapping his claws around a pair of chains dangling from the ceiling and swinging happily.

I follow. Reach for him.

With a pleased *"Karaaa Kraaa,"* Kitten takes flight again. Zooming under the torture rack, he finds another swinging metal object I don't want to know the use of. Clings to it. Throws back his tiny horns and happily lets loose a victorious flame, casting dancing shadows all over the stone.

"Goddammit!"

"Stop chasing him," Asher says. "He thinks it's a game."

Yes, he does. "What if we come at him together? Herd him from both sides toward the door?"

Asher's shoulders tighten slightly as he moves deeper into the room, but he obediently takes the back left corner as I set up on the right. Pulling off his black sweater, Asher waits for my signal before windmilling the cloth in a figure-eight pattern as we both move toward the dragon.

"*Kraaaaaaa!*" Kitten screeches as he takes flight, belching a string of fire to let us know his displeasure at this turn of events. *"Kraaaaaa! Kraaaa! Kraaaaa!"*

Exchanging a determined glance, Asher and I press on, Kitten now zooming about like a deranged pigeon, flapping wings and spitting flames. My pulse beats hard and steady, adrenaline coursing through my veins. The little dragon might be unhappy, but he is also moving. Closing in on the door. A few more steps and we'll get him out of here.

"Once he's out, cut off the route to the right," Asher orders. "We don't need him going deeper."

"Will do." I take another step. Another. Three more and we will be in the clear. Two more.

Asher snaps his sweater in the air, and Kitten twirls around, snapping back at the fabric. Tongues of fire whirl with him, already so close to the door that they scorch the metal grating, running down the metal bars like a parlor trick.

…right into the old wooden wedge that Asher stuck beneath the door.

As if struck by lightning, the dry old doorstop erupts in flames, even Kitten recoiling from the sudden burst.

"Kitten," I yell desperately, watching as the tip of one wing catches in the grating—the other flapping frantically.

Billowing the flames even higher.

"The door!" Asher hollers. I freeze in place, watching in horror as Kitten's twisting about makes the door teeter precariously. Out and in. Out and in, in, in. Each swing of the grating agitates the panicked dragon more. More fire belches from him, red and white and orange tongues that cocoon him in an illusion of safety.

Ignoring the flames and the iron in the bars, Asher dives for the closing gate. The tips of his fingers slide across the floor, reaching the teetering door one moment too late.

I hear the fateful click of a lock and feel ice slide down my spine. We're trapped.

23

—————

ASHER

*T*he deafening sound of the lock clicking into place echoed through Asher's body. He dared not check the door, though, not until the dragon—who'd somehow gotten his wing trapped between the iron bars in his panic—finally extricated himself and soared to pout on the opposite side of the interrogation chamber.

Asher tried to keep his breathing even as he rose from the stone floor, tried to give no outward sign how quickly his heart galloped inside his chest. Everything here smelled wrong, from the old tang of dried blood to the fresh stench of burned flesh that streaked over his forearm, to the dank must of the stone walls that seemed to close around him on all sides. Reaching for the door, Asher ignored the sting of iron as he gave the grating a hard yank.

It didn't budge, the old mechanism having clicked deviously into place.

"I take it you don't have a key?" Samantha asked.

Asher gave the witch a sideways glance. "I wasn't planning on coming here."

And yet here he was, locked in a dungeon cell with a witch. Again. A witch as breathtaking as Sienna had been. More. Asher's body betrayed him at the sight of Samantha no matter what he did, no matter how much he hated his own physiology for it. There was something about her full lips and fuller breasts, the curve of her hips, the intelligent eyes that went from vulnerable to hardened and back again in a span of a blink, that made his cock ache even now. Which was really, *really* inconvenient right at this moment.

"Hello!" Samantha raised her voice, hollering into the void. "Can anyone hear us?"

"They can't." Reaching into his pocket, Asher pulled out his cell phone. No reception. He hadn't expected any down here, but it still stung. "I don't think anyone will come looking until neither of us turns up for morning formation tomorrow."

Jake. Asher braced his hand on the stone wall, his chest tightening. He'd promised the boy he would be back in an hour. The first damn promise he'd made to his son, he was going to break. And in the worst possible way.

"With where your room is, someone will explore the passages in all directions," Asher continued, his voice too calm for the throbbing tension in his gut. "Looking here may not be the first course of investigation, but it will make the list."

Sam shuddered. Because no sane creature would be at ease trapped inside a torture chamber? Or because she feared spending time in Asher's company in particular? Either way, her vulnerability only heightened Asher's discomfort. In her clingy old T-shirt and blue jersey pajama pants, she looked younger, softer. She looked like Sam behind closed doors, the one he'd never been privy to until now.

"I can try the opening spell," she said quietly, curling protectively around herself as a new wave of fear trickled into her scent. She didn't want to do what she offered. Feared it. "The one I used on Ellis's shackles."

"The one that brought the whole chemistry lab down on your head the last time you tried it?" Asher said, looking at the ceiling. He didn't know the structure of the dungeon well enough, but the possibility of a tunnel collapse blocking the route all together was high enough. "Let's leave that option for a last resort."

Retrieving his sweater—which had somehow survived the ordeal intact—Asher found the least soiled corner of the room and laid the woolen fabric down on the stone beside him. "Come here." He patted the seat. "You're already shivering."

Sam advanced toward him warily, like a feral cub.

"If you let yourself get too cold, it will be that much more difficult to warm up," he said reasonably, convincing himself as much as her that this was the right thing to do. *Objectively* right, and not just because each of Sam's shivers ratcheted Asher's protective instinct up another notch, until it was all he could do to keep from grabbing her and pulling her against him. "It won't mean you forgive me."

With a final hesitation, Sam settled tightly beside him, unable to lean her back against the wall the way he could. With a sigh, Asher nudged her against his side, settling the protest with a firm hand wrapped around the girl's shoulders —above the level of her wounds.

"You're cold and you're hurt, both of which happened at my hand," he said quietly into her hair, willing his body to ignore how perfectly she fit into the groove of his shoulder, the way her sweet citrusy scent calmed his nerves the way nothing ever had. Even as it raised his pulse. Fucking hell. Maybe it was because he was already on edge from being trapped here, but Sam's very scent stretched his control to the limit. "You can still hate me when we get out of here, but you *will* let me offer what comfort I can just now."

Sam's scent spiked at the command, a hint of arousal and defiance that he couldn't parse out against his own confused senses. All he knew was that the feel of Sam's soft, warm flesh pressing against him chased away a fog inside his soul.

The tense silence between them beat out time in heartbeats, until the fatigue in Sam's body finally drained enough of her strength that she closed her eyes, falling into a light sleep against his chest. He didn't dare move. Not after an hour or three. Not even when his leg started to cramp from staying in one place. The caress of Sam's trust as she let her guard down enough to sleep against him was too valuable to risk disturbing.

It was sometime around midnight when Sam roused again. She woke slowly, still leaning against him, rubbing her face as she got her bearings.

Asher tightened his hold, a soft invite to stay beside him, and felt a shot of relief when she accepted.

"Is this the kind of place Sienna held you in?" Sam asked.

"Of all the things to ask, that one seemed like a good idea right now?"

"It came to mind." Sam sucked a breath. "And it was feeling too quiet in here."

"All right. A question for a question, then." The words had tumbled from Asher's lips without a filter, but—surprisingly— he didn't regret it. There was a kind of freedom in talking to Sam right now that he hadn't felt with anyone but the horsemen—but even that was different. "It was somewhat like it. But better hidden and bigger. Enough to hold all four of us and a whole laboratory of potions and spell aids." He swallowed, feeling the tug to hear more of her voice. To learn more about her. "My turn, then. Where did you live before the

Academy? Bryant just sent you to my doorstep. He didn't bother to include any paperwork."

"New Jersey." Sam shimmied for a better position against his side, oblivious to what her squirming did to his pulse. "I was in the foster system for as long as I can remember and had just escaped the state's system when I ran into Ellis."

Asher sucked in a breath, suppressing the pang of jealousy at the way Sam uttered Ellis's name.

"My turn," she said, picking up the rules he himself had laid down. "Why do you hate Cassis?"

"Because…" Asher paused, the answer he'd had on the tip of his tongue no longer feeling right. What business was it of his that Cassis made a mockery of the discipline he himself clung to, or that the vamp wasted his great talents as a warrior and healer on debauchery? If Cassis was happy, who gave Asher the right to begrudge him that? "Because I'm an asshole."

Sam snorted.

Asher breathed in her scent, savoring it inside him. "What specifically happened during the punishment?" He held his breath. He needed to hear the whole of it. Needed her to know that he heard, that he understood what he'd done to her.

She tensed. "You were there, sir."

"You don't have to call me that right now," said Asher. "For God's sake, we've just managed to get ourselves locked in a dungeon cell."

Sam pushed away from him, that fire he'd missed sparking in her hazel eyes. "You're the one who just reminded me of what happens when I cross you. I wouldn't want to get out of the habit of proper address and face your wrath later."

Yes. That was it, that note of life and defiance that made Samantha who she was. This was the Samantha who'd made Reese feel alive for the first time in centuries—who was now doing the same to him. Asher locked eyes with Sam's gaze, his heart speeding. "Now you care about my wrath?" he asked, egging her on, feeding that flame of life and rebellion that he'd come criminally close to destroying. "Frankly, I didn't think six cuts would make that much of an impression."

"Don't give yourself that much credit." Sam sucked in a breath, her chest heaving as she stared at him in challenge. Heat radiating from the witch's body brushed over Asher's face, stirring his cock, her full, half-open lips ripe for the taking.

"Who does get the credit?" Asher said, recklessly undoing all the discipline that had once seemed so damn important to him. "I might want to send a thank-you note."

"Asshole."

"Hoodlum."

"Egotistical. Domineering. Male." Sam's words came one at a time, her scent filling Asher's lungs.

Asher leaned over her. Breathed in the sweet, citrusy lemongrass. "Witch," he snarled into Sam's face, and sealed his lips over hers.

24

SAM

*A*sher's mouth closes around mine, the hot force of his kiss racing through every fiber of my body. Need rushes through me like a wave, waking my sex and breasts and mouth to the male's sandalwood scent. There's nothing gentle about his kiss, nothing soft about his tongue deeply pillaging my mouth. My thighs moisten at the feel of the intense connection that I've wanted and denied wanting and hated wanting for so damn long. Magic coils within me, threatening to awaken my senses, and my fear of the coming pain makes my heart pound harder, even as my need compresses like a coiled spring.

I twist my hands through Asher's golden hair, my mouth pressing back against his. My heart pounds, my sex pulsing hungrily. But I can't do this. Not with a male who tore Ellis from me. Who destroyed Mika's lifeline to information. Who split the flesh along my back with the same ruthless efficiency that he's done everything else. Asher is a power-hungry male, like so many I've met.

Moisture slips from my aching sex, my need little caring for my thoughts. Kitten's soft clanking sounds in the far corner fade into the background, all my nerves narrowing in on Asher's delicious, spicy taste. I meet the savage kiss head-on, retaliating with every forceful slide of my mouth, going head-to-head with the powerful male.

"You are a fucking bastard," I hiss as our lips separate. The loss of the connection makes my nerves scream with dissatisfaction. My breaths come in short heaves as I inhale the stale must of the cool dungeon and the clashing sandalwood warmth. "I hate you."

"You should," Asher growls into my face. Specks of gold dance in his irises like sparks.

Twisting onto my knees, my channel blazing with heat, I seal my mouth over his lips and pillage him savagely. My nails rake down his arms, breaking skin. I want to fight him. Hurt him. Take him. I want to feel alive, and damn it, Asher's unyielding hold on the back of my head fans those flames.

Letting go of his hair, I plunge my hand down to the pulsing bulge inside his jeans.

The male arches, desperate groans escaping into my mouth. Yes. He felt that.

I pull my head back, watching Asher struggle to breathe, and suddenly know exactly what I want.

Stroking Asher's erection, I grip his tawny gaze, savor his glassy eyes as his body vibrates beneath my touch. His cock pulsates against his jeans, his body wanting to respond. Sheathed violence and desperation all wash over his chiseled tense face. And vulnerability too. Maybe neither one of us is ready for this.

"You're locked in a dungeon with a witch," I hiss into Asher's ear, yanking down his zipper. "How does that feel, you asshole?"

Asher shakes his head, escaping my gaze, his eyes

shuddering. His hands curl at his sides along the stone. Holding himself from pouncing on me as his freed cock springs from his jeans. Large and thick and deliciously velvety. It's so long that it curves slightly, the bead of moisture on its tip begging to be licked off.

My mouth waters.

"Stand up and put your palms on the wall," I tell Asher. My order is hoarse, and he flinches as I deliver it.

Uncurling powerfully to his feet, the male stands with his legs apart, leaning forward to press his palms against the stone. With his body angled this way, his cock is at the perfect level for me to do what I wish. And damn it, I intend to.

Cupping the warm base of Asher's shaft, I lick that bead of moisture on the head first, savoring the delicious maleness. Shit. Just that little taste of him sends blazing heat along my nerves, making my clit tingle. I lick him again, savoring the salty taste before taking him deep into my mouth. The warm, living cock inside me pulses desperately, Asher's body trembling beneath every lick and suckle as I work my mouth up and down the shaft. Pleasure fills my mouth, and I suck ruthlessly, imagining that I can pull him dry.

Asher's whole body shifts from fine trembles to frantic spasms, his knees buckling. Another hard suckle and the *twitch twitch twitch* of the cock against my tongue morphs to desperate jerks, small sounds escaping between his clenched teeth. Looking up, I see his face pale with need, his hands bone white as he presses them against the cold stone. Vulnerable. Desperate. Out of control.

I lick his cock again and pull away, power flowing through me, and he gasps. My own sex pulses along with Asher's, the mere thought of tasting the load I know is near almost sending me over the edge. I cup his tight, heavy sac, my thumb brushing the coarse hairs.

"Samantha." The plea in Asher's voice makes me flush.

Taking him inside me, I suck the shaft as deep into my mouth as I wish, pulling on his wonderful saltiness over and over until it fills my mouth in concert to Asher's primal shouts of release. The thick seed spills blissfully into my mouth and throat, every drop filling me with energy and power and need. Asher's sounds echo off the stone, spurring Kitten into fire-belching flight.

As the last spasm gripping Asher finishes, his muscles give out. Sliding down to the cold ground, he grips both sides of my head with his callused palms and kisses me thoroughly. Deeply. A zing of warmth flows from my mouth to my breasts and sex and skin. On the heels of swallowing his seed, with my channel keening to be filled, the claiming kiss explodes through me.

Crashes into the coiled power of my magic.

I gasp, fear rolling through me at the thought of magic spilling into my blood and waking my senses like it did during the lashing.

"What is it?" Asher whispers when I try to pull away, his eyes penetrating deep into me. And this time, I can't help it. I tell him the truth. About what happened. About the coiled magic I'm afraid to give release to now. About being afraid how much it will hurt to feel every injured fiber of my body. About the ancient memories that the pain plunged me into.

I brace myself to be called coward, but Asher stares at me as if he'd just been slugged. "I didn't know," he whispers. "Didn't even suspect the nightmares."

"And if you had?"

"I'd never have let you leave my study without finding a way to ease it." Leaning toward me, Asher brushes his lips over mine. "When Ellis was hurt, you pulled the iron from him by connecting the marks?" he asks.

I nod, confusion flooding my hazy mind.

Nodding, Asher rips open the left sleeve of his shirt. "Then I wager it works both ways, witch," he says. His voice is harsh, filled with protectiveness. Before I can process what's happening, he takes my scared palm and presses that star-shaped burn against the star Sienna left forearm.

Like a plug closing an electrical circuit, the connection between Asher and me is immediate and potent, my magic releasing from its spring-loaded trap at the same time.

My senses waken, my nose smelling the full bouquet off rust and mildew around us, my ears hearing each slight sound down to the soft creak of the iron manacle that Kitten disturbed in his flight. But most of all, I feel that horrid agony along my back, the split skin and blood and—and then I don't, as if the pain is sucked away from me, leaving only a slight warm throbbing behind.

I gasp, staring at Asher's face. There's a glaze of pain over his eyes. My pain. The one he called to himself through our growing connection, which now pulses with a protectiveness I know is his.

"No." I shake my head. "You can't take my pain."

"I can, and I will." Asher says with steely force, pulling my shirt over my head to free my breasts. Quickly spreading his discarded sweater over the stone, he pushes my back down onto it.

I brace for the jolt of pain, but nothing comes, only a slight flinch on Asher's face as he cups my breasts. "Do not let go of my mark," he orders, the demand jetting through me and right down to my clit.

"But—"

Asher clamps his hand over mine, keeping our marks connected. My magic flares, twining with the immortal essence inside Asher, the two twisting around each other like vines.

Lowering his face to me, Asher nips the top of my ear. "I think you need something else to focus on."

Before I can move, the male takes my bunched nipple into his mouth and sucks.

My body arches toward him. Heat sears through my heavy breast, the slight scrape of Asher's canine delicately skirting the edge of pain and danger before morphing to molten heat. Bracing himself over me, Asher circles his tongue leisurely around the peak, then does the same with my other breast.

My dripping sex clenches, waves of arousal raking through my body. I'm panting by the time he releases my nipples, the moist nipples puckered against the air.

Asher grazes a finger down my abdomen to the waistline of my pants, the heat of his body cocooning me from the dungeon's chill.

With a powerful yank that takes my pants and panties off in a single pull, he bares me to him. Coolness brushes my hot folds and then his hand is there stroking possessively up and down, up and down, until I am writhing with the need for more friction. My hips buck, the ache around my swollen clit making my back spasm.

Wrapping his hands beneath my thighs, Asher hoists my legs onto his shoulder, folding me in half beneath his great size. I feel the thick head of his cock swirl around my entrance as his finger traces my hood, flicking left and right, left and right, until the engorged bud screams through my whole body.

I gasp, digging my nails into Asher's back. In the distance, Kitten's joyful *kraa kraa* bounces off the stone walls, his wings whispering against the air as he soars around the room. Through the soft sweater, stones dig into my back. Yet all my focus is on the wet pulsing of my sex, the feel of Asher's thick cock so, so close to plunging into me. Any moment now. Any heartbeat. I whimper, biting my lips to keep from begging him to take me. Just when I'm certain I can't last another moment, my hips bucking in reckless abandon, I finally feel the full length of Asher's thick cock slide into me. He fills me completely. Perfectly. So deep at this angle, that for a moment, I can't breathe.

My magic flares, my channel stretching to accommodate his great size as he pulls back and thrusts again, harder, striking a spot so shockingly deep inside me that I let loose a breathy scream. Then he's moving. Each thrust giving no mercy. Again. And again. And again. He pounds into me faster now, eliciting primal sounds I've never heard myself make before. My toes curl, my heart jackhammering against my chest. I'm pinned to the floor, all my nerve endings narrowed in on my drenched swollen sex being pummeled by Asher's hard length. His sculpted face is tense with restrained wildness, a single vein pulsing on his forehead, his tawny eyes misted over.

The rhythmic *thump thump thump* of Asher's sac against my ass echoes off the silent walls, mingling with our harsh breaths. Over and over, each perfect thrust raising me closer to the edge of an abyss. I feel the pounding of Asher's heart all through my body, from his throbbing cock to the throbbing magic resonating through us both. Consuming everything.

Returning to my clit, Asher teases the bud mercilessly, scraping the callused pad of his thumb along the sensitive flesh. I'm keening helplessly now, Kitten joining in my cries, every inch of my body trembling as I rise toward an impossibly explosive release. Up and up and up.

I gasp for breath, holding onto Asher's arm and riveting gaze. The tawny eyes looking back at me penetrate right through my soul. Each thrust tangles our magics closer together, cinching the bond between us. Even here, in the darkness of the dungeon, I know that something about this coupling is different.

We aren't fucking.

We're mating.

I gasp at the realization as fear and apprehension and need flood through me, the same emotions flashing across Asher's face.

He knows too. Feels what the plunge into the gaping abyss will mean.

My heart pounds, my breath misting the air between us to the pulsing of his impossibly large cock.

Hooking my waist with one arm, Asher suddenly sits back on his haunches and yanks my hips up into the air, his muscles bunching like a predator about to pounce.

"Samantha?" he shouts in demand and question. Throwing me one final lifeline, though I know, through our magic, that stopping now would tear Asher's soul apart.

"Yes," I pant.

And that's all it takes. Asher looses the deepest, most powerful thrust yet. The thick head of his cock angles, striking me right on that spot deep inside that's the nexus of every nerve and fiber.

My muscles bunch as waves of release mercilessly take over my body, the pleasure so fierce that it borders on pain. As my channel clenches around Asher's rigid length, I feel his seed spill inside me, driving me into another orgasm with a deep, guttural moan. The waves of desperate pleasure crash again and again until all my strength is gone and I'm puddled on the ground, holding on to my mate for all I'm worth.

"I still don't like you," I whisper, my mouth dry from the panting, my world still swimming from the orgasms that took me over completely. Oh fuck. My body feels like it's running on magic alone, every fiber too spent and extorted to continue existing.

"I don't much care for you either, witch," Asher whispers back, curling tighter around me on the floor. His hand stays over mine, careful to ensure that I don't let our marks separate even for a moment as he buries his face in my hair, taking deep breaths while I tremble against him. "But I love you nonetheless."

The words come in such a thin whisper that I'm not sure I heard correctly, except that my magic heats in acknowledgment of them. As Asher brushes his lips against my neck, something inside me heaves a big sigh and relaxes, as if a missing piece of my soul has finally snapped into place.

ASHER

$\mathcal{A}$sher cradled Sam on his lap, her body soft and content in the afterthroes of release, and felt complete for the first time in centuries. For the first time in his life, if he were being honest with himself. Leaning back against the wall, he breathed in Samantha's sweet citrus scent, each lungful settling like a balm inside his lungs. Steadying him. Giving him strength.

A mate. Holy hell. Holy fucking hell.

The sensation was so all-consuming, Asher understood why Victor had gone to such lengths to try to prevent this happening. Now that Asher had mated with Samantha body and soul, he was never going to let her go. Not for the Academy. Not for the world.

Sam stirred, turning her large hazel eyes up at him. "Well." She cleared her throat. "This isn't exactly what I was expecting."

"No. Not at all." Asher snorted softly. "I'm not sure how I'm supposed to kick myself off campus now, to keep from having an overprotective mate hovering around one cadet and all." He meant the words lightly, but Samantha's face tensed at once, those intelligent eyes hitting him deep down.

He felt her body shift and grabbed her wrist, lest her hand come off where the mark connected them. Drawing her physical pain to himself was easy now that Asher had gotten the hang of the connection, though it was harder to keep his own experiences with Sienna from flooding the bond the other way.

"We can't just stay like this forever," Sam said, her voice too reasonable. Too brave for her own good. "I'm going to have to let go sooner or later."

"Later," Asher said.

"That's not a plan. That's procrastination."

He closed his eyes, resting his forehead against Sam's head. She was right. But he couldn't bear it. "Just until I tend to the wounds, then."

Sitting up carefully and pulling the little witch into his lap, Asher ripped his shirt into long strips and wrapped them around her torso. Admittedly, doing this before their recent activity would have been more on point, but obviously, that ship had long since sailed. Sam shifted to get more comfortable, and Asher's cock stirred beneath her, ready to forget reality and explore the mating bond all over again.

How in the hell had Ellis managed? How had he allowed Asher to separate him from his mate? If the situation were reversed, Asher was certain he'd have ripped his brother's throat out. Or tried to.

"Before you go back to being an unbearable asshole tomorrow…" Sam said, her voice hitching unexpectedly on the last word. Frowning, she shook her head as if clearing a fog. "Never mind. I forgot what I was going to say."

"Something about my being an unbearable asshole," Asher

prompted, watching her face. "Or something about tomorrow."

There. It happened again. A small flinch. A tiny shiver along the newly formed mating bond.

"What's important about tomorrow?" Asher pressed.

Beneath his hands, Sam's pulse began to pound along her ribs, vibrating the bond of magic between them.

"Nothing," she snapped, pulling away from him.

The witch's voice was determined enough that Asher simply would have assumed the events of the last hour were finally catching up with her higher reasoning—except for the line of connection still flowing through the bond between them. The feeling of something wrong crawled down his spine as he tried and failed to grip Samantha's eyes with his own. He clamped his hand over her wrist, getting there just in time to keep the witch from severing the connection. "Let me go," she insisted. "It's nothing. I want to tell you nothing."

She was lying. Except she wasn't.

Closing his eyes, Asher focused all his energy on Samantha's inner turmoil. The physical pain, which he'd been pulling into himself, was reduced to a distant throb, her senses calming after overwhelming arousal. Except there was something else rippling along the magic now, a cord of anxiety twisting in her chest that repelled all attempts to touch it.

"Samantha," Asher said slowly, "I think you are under a compulsion."

She yanked her hand hard, and Asher let it go, his chest tightening as she flinched at the sudden pain. "Damn it," she cursed, her gaze narrowing. "That hurts. You hurt me." Sam stepped away from him, backing toward the other side of the cell.

Asher's neck tensed, his mind spinning even as his body and soul mourned the distance she was now putting between them. "Samantha," he asked quietly. "What vampires were you alone with today?"

"None." She swallowed. "I mean… I don't want to talk about it."

"No, I bet you don't." Asher rubbed his eyes with the heel of his hand. Damn it. If he'd been paying less attention to his cock and more to the bond between them, he might have felt the problem sooner. "Can I take your pain for a little longer?" he asked, choosing his words carefully. "I imagine we'll be here"—he swallowed the word *tomorrow* which seemed to be a trigger—"for a while still. The ache is easier for me to bear. In fact, I think the immortal magic inside me helps your flesh knit together."

Sam took a step toward him. Stopped. Shook her head. "You want to get into my head. You want to take my thoughts against my will, Asher." Her voice rose. "Tell me I'm wrong."

"You are wrong." *It's not* your *will I'm trying to overcome.* It was all he could do to keep his voice calm, the protective instinct inside him roaring in fury. Someone was trying to control his mate. That someone was going to die.

Sam's steps quickened, turning to a desperate pacing that worried Asher more with every moment.

Gathering all his willpower, he forced his body to lean back against the stone. The one good thing about compulsion was that it faded with time. Whatever was happening, tomorrow would be a better time to deal with it. "You know what," he said, yawning as he shimmied into a better position, "it doesn't matter. Let's sleep for a bit. I think we both could use the rest."

2 6

SAM

I wake to the sound of soft voices and lift my head from where it's pillowed on Asher's muscled thigh. I blink into the darkness, my body struggling to orient itself. I'm in the dungeon, lying on the cold stone, Kitten curled behind my knees. The stinker is the one responsible for Asher and me getting trapped here. But what happened afterward—the sex, the *mating*—that was all us. Holy hell.

"What time is it?" I ask.

Asher strokes my hair, trailing his fingers very gently down my back. "About five in the morning. Fortunately, Reese decided against waiting until morning formation to come looking for us. You can rest a bit more while he's getting the keys."

I nod sleepily, savoring the feel of Asher's body beneath me. Though if memory serves, he wasn't in his fae form the whole night. Pushing myself up, I look down at my clothes and find strands of golden-white wolf hair covering my pants. Seeing me pick up the evidence of his shedding, Asher turns his face away, the tips of his ears coloring slightly.

"Things appear to have changed," Reese says when he returns, the rusty door opening with an irate groan. Despite the tension coming off his quiet body, his attention is fully on Asher as the latter pulls on his sweater, taking more time than necessary to adjust it along his muscled abdomen. Discomfort shimmers around him, but when I try to step away, he slips his arm around my shoulders, pulling me toward him. "They have," he tells Reese, raising his chin. "Things have changed a great deal, brother."

Reesand draws one of his rare breaths. *Brother.* Because, like both Reese and Ellis, Asher and I are now tied together, a shared bond that connects the three of them on a whole new level. Deep in my gut, I know Cassis is destined to be a part of us as well. But I'm not sure how to bring that up. Especially because Reese has still not looked at me. My stomach tightens.

"How is Jake?" Asher asks.

"He wasn't happy when you failed to return last night," Reese said flatly. "Food seems to go a long way toward soothing hurt feelings, though. He's asleep in your bed."

"Thank you. I should be there to wake him." Asher slips his hand to the base of my neck, rubbing a small circle. Now that things have shifted between us, he seems to need the reassurance of physical contact as much as I do. "Then I'll call Ellis over, and we can talk."

"And Cassis," I say.

Asher's jaw tightens, something like a mix of possession and jealousy flashing in his eyes, but he nods. "Cassis too." He turns to Reese. "Can you watch over Samantha until then?"

"Bring celery to the meeting," I call after Asher, not altogether certain that I came to that idea entirely on my own. When I turn to glare at Kitten, however, the dragon piously takes flight.

With nothing more to distract me from Reese's cold

shoulder, I fall into step beside him, the chilly dawn's silence stretching between us. "Why didn't you come to me when you were hurt?" he asks finally. "Did you doubt I'd care for you?"

I flinch at the hurt in his voice, the memory of exactly how skilled he is at taking care of me flooding my blood.

"You didn't seem too keen on fraternization last time I saw you," I snap back. I shake my head. "I wanted some privacy."

"Did you?" He sounds unimpressed.

"Yes. Habit of my upbringing." I follow the vampire into the infirmary and skirt around the exam room to go straight into his private office, daring him to say something. To treat me like just another patient. Like just another cadet.

Reese follows me in. Closes the door. For a moment, nothing happens, then the vamp moves faster than I can follow, jetting in front of me to grip my face and tilt it up toward him.

"It's a habit I intend to break." Reese's low, gravelly voice matches his beautiful face. He looms over me, his body taking over my world as his penetrating blue eyes bore into me. My heart quickens, jolts of heat racing through me. Waking me. Turning my knees to Jell-O.

Reese's thumb traces my cheekbone, the callused pad scraping intimately along my skin. His ocean scent washes over me, bringing memories. All sorts of memories. I swallow, unable to look away as my pulse races inside my chest.

Reese's dark brow twitches, as if he can read my thoughts. Or scent them. Bastard.

Either way, the broody male has me trapped in his gaze, holding me there for heartbeat after heartbeat while the tension crackles around us, singeing the air. "Hide from me again, Samantha, and I will tan your arse," he says into my ear, his voice soft and menacing. And hot enough to make moisture slide down the insides of my thighs. "I'd do it now if we didn't have other things to worry about."

My face heats, my cheeks surely turning all shades of red from Reese's threat. From my body's treacherous response. "Fucking bastard," I whisper, my voice hoarse. "You win."

"I always win," he replies, his lips lowering to mine, his sea-breeze scent washing over me.

My mouth opens to him, not that Reese would allow anything different. His kiss is deep and claiming, his tongue pillaging my mouth with punishing force. And fuck me, I love him for it, for knowing that no amount of gentleness would reassure me the way this does right now.

My soul wakens to him, every fiber of my body alert despite the early hour as I savor him. And then I'm kissing him back with all my desperate might, gripping the tight muscles at his waist, digging my fingers into him hard enough to bruise a mortal.

Someone clears his throat behind us.

Giving my lip a final nip, Reese lifts his head away to glare at the interruption. Turning toward the door, I discover that Asher has returned—and that Reese has no intention of letting me go.

Asher snorts. "This is going to be a hell of an interesting day. I brought Sam some clothes, by the way."

Asher's *interesting* prediction proves true an hour later when Ellis strides into the infirmary, takes one nostrils-flaring sniff, and wheels on Asher, murder flashing in his golden eyes.

Snagging the last of the celery Asher brought along, Kitten industriously takes it to the top of the bookshelf, wet chewing sounds doing little to dispel the brewing tension.

"I smell witch blood." Ellis's words vibrate off the walls as he stalks toward his brother. "What did you do to her?"

Before Asher can answer, the air around Ellis shimmers,

the fae male shifting into a snarling white wolf. Reese wraps an arm around me at once, yanking me back just as Asher shifts as well, his white-and-gold wolf no less primal than Ellis's.

The two predators circle each other, their salivating canines bared, tails straight and hackles high. Ellis's snow-white wolf crouches back on his hindquarters and pounces. Deadly jaws close on Asher's neck.

My breath halts.

Asher's wolf lets loose a sound between a yip and a growl, twisting his lithe, powerful body, returning the assault. In the blink of an eye, the pair is tumbling on the floor in a ball of fur and teeth, knocking over a stack of Reese's files. The avalanche of paper slides to the ground, making at least one of the wolves tuck his tail for a moment before launching into a new assault.

I see specks of blood mat someone's fur, but can't tell whose it is in the shifting tumble until the pair separate and circle each other, teeth snapping at tails.

"Oh, for fuck's sake!" Stalking up to the pair, I grab the first tail my hand manages to close around and yank. Hard.

The wolf in question—who I think is Ellis—twists around in indignation, snapping his teeth at me, yellow eyes blazing.

My heart stutters for a second, but I know deep down that neither of the wolves will injure me. Not truly. Without stopping to consider what *truly injure* might mean to an immortal wolf, I give the tail in question another hard yank and insert myself between the two brawlers.

"Stop this nonsense," I say, bracing my fists on my hips. "What are you, twelve?"

The wolves turn their snarling muzzles toward me. I stare right back at them, my magic waking. The buzzing bees are closer to the surface than they've ever been before. My back stings, a hundred different smells assaulting my nose. Old paper, ink from the ancient pen Reese favors, caustic cleaning agents wafting in from the exam room next door, the tang heavy enough to leave a coat of bitterness along my mouth.

With a dismissive growl, the wolves turn back toward each other. Circling. Readying for attack.

My magic rakes through the room, instinct taking the reins from reason. Looking for something. I feel the heat of the sun's rays streaming through the window onto the floor at the same time that I realize their utility. Focusing on the sun's warmth, I feed my magic into the rays in a single short burst.

A heartbeat later, the wooden floor right in the center of the wolves' brawl erupts in flames.

The wolves jump back, shifting to their fae form.

Reese grabs a fire extinguisher from the wall. Before anyone can speak, the vamp turns the hose first on the fire, and then on all three of us. "Anyone else have any brilliant ideas to try out in my workroom?" he asks.

My face heats. "I'm good."

Wrapping his arm around my waist, Ellis pulls me possessively toward him. "We're fine."

Asher's chest heaves, the bloodied spot on his shoulder revealing who was on the losing end of the fight before I broke it up. Throwing Ellis a glare, he grabs a chair for himself and sits. "We're fine," he echoes.

"Lovely," says Reese, putting out the final ember of the flame before stowing the fire extinguisher. "I'm glad we've settled that."

"Almost settled." Putting his hands on the crests of my hips, Ellis spins me around to face him. With his legs spread wide apart, he is as deadly and beautiful as I remember, his shiny white hair loose around his shoulders. Bringing a finger up to my face, the male hooks a lock of hair slowly behind my ear. "You are one troublemaking witch, Devinee," he says, lowering his face toward mine until I see the specks of gold dancing majestically in his yellow eyes. "And that is exactly the way I love you."

My breath halts as Ellis's lips brush mine with unexpected gentleness.

I rise onto my toes, giving myself into the kiss, savoring the warmth flowing through me as the connection deepens. Ellis's hands slide down my sides. Brush the curve of my hips. Dip to my waistband and—

"If I'd known it was this kind of party, I'd have come earlier," Cassis says from the door.

SAM

I cringe. Ellis does not.

As if not having heard the vampire, he proceeds to trace his hand all around the low waistline of my jeans, his mouth continuing a similar exploration against my own.

"Cassis," Ellis says finally as the kiss ends, his attention never straying from my face. "If *I* knew it was this sort of party, I'd have ensured you weren't invited."

Cassis closes the door and scans the room with an unamused gaze. There's something about my friend that feels off, a tension that vibrates the air around him. I pull against Ellis's hold, and the male loosens it at once, his hands still draped around my hips but no longer trapping me in place.

"Cassis." I take a step toward him, but the vampire only nods his greeting before striding forward to grab an empty chair. Turning it around, he straddles it as if riding a horse. He's uncharacteristically casual today in a long-sleeved white shirt that hugs every one of his muscles and slim-cut black jeans. This may be the first time I'm seeing him in something other than a suit—and, I realize with a jolt, it's the first time I'm seeing him in the daytime.

"This looks like an intervention gathering," he says lazily. "What exactly are the horsemen intervening on?"

Horsemen. Yes. What the four of them once called themselves, before a witch tore their souls apart. The word permeates through the room, chilling the air to match Cassis's cool tone.

Asher clears his throat, surveying everyone one more time before speaking. "I mated with Samantha," he says. "The bond snapped into place last night."

"Good for you," says Cassis. "I'll have a cake sent over."

"That makes at least three of us," Asher continues, as Ellis runs his hand possessively down my arm. "Ellis. Reesand. Me."

"So why the bloody hell am I at this party?" Cassis says, never glancing my way. A pang of hurt races through me, but I push it aside. Whatever I feel is a fraction of the torment that seems to be raking through his soul, and my not understanding what's happening inside him makes it no less real.

"You are here because Samantha asked that you be," Asher says.

My breath halts. I wait for Cassis to turn toward me, but he doesn't.

"She made a mistake," he says instead, getting up off his chair and starting for the door. "Why don't you and your new *mate* try to figure out what to do next without my sage advice. I've got missing humans to recover."

"There's something else," Asher calls after Cassis. "I think Samantha is under compulsion."

I twist toward the fae, an irrational anxiety rushing through me. I'd thought we put that argument to bed last night, but it seems Asher was simply laying a trap. I'm not under compulsion. I can't be. *Missing humans, missing humans, missing humans.* Cassis's last words replay themselves in my mind, each spurring my heart to a faster beat. *Missing humans, missing humans, missing humans.*

Cassis stop. Turns. Bares his fangs. "You think I compelled Samantha?"

Behind me, Ellis tenses, a growl rumbling through his chest. "Did you?"

"Stop!" *Missing humans, missing humans, missing humans.* I draw a breath, a feat harder than it should be. "Cassis can't compel me. Neither can Reese. It doesn't work." I rub my face, trying to reclaim agency over my own thoughts. Maybe the males are right, though I don't understand how such a thing would be possible. "I didn't even speak with a full vampire yesterday."

Cassis's gaze narrows, and for the first time since coming into the room, the whole of his attention focuses on me. "Can you account for every part of the day yesterday?" he asks.

"Of course."

"Indulge me," he says.

I hold up my hand, raising fingers one at a time. "Morning formation. Breakfast. Work detail. Going to Asher's office for um…"

"Punishment," Asher supplies, the other males in the room tensing.

"Punishment," I echo quickly. "Then I went back to my room." I blink, frowning. I remember going to my room and I remember being there, but the journey itself is a strange blur. "I don't remember actually getting there or changing," I say slowly. "Though obviously, both things happened. Is amnesia part of compulsion?"

"Not like this," says Reese. "Presuming Samantha *was* compelled during that time, and that the timing was not coincidental, what would she have been most predisposed to want just then? What would have been the opportune button to press?"

"After I'd just whipped her?" says Asher. "Frankly, it would have been a grand time to suggest that I'm an asshole who should be eviscerated."

Reese shakes his head. "Unless Samantha was predisposed to enjoy evisceration, such a compulsion would never work. Compulsion can be potent, but it still leverages suggestion. It can't turn someone into a blind murderer."

"I'm not supposed to be unable to remember anything either." I wrap my arms around myself. "Plus, shouldn't its power have faded by now?"

"When did the lot of you become so bloody naïve?" Cassis asks with genuine curiosity. "You think that just because Ellis decides to hide in Talon for a few centuries and Asher is so rule abiding that the stick up his arse is coming out his mouth, the rest of the world stays still? Even humans have developed plenty of chemical agents to keep them company—you think vampires are any different?"

Silence. Asher looks away.

Pulling me over to him, Cassis takes my chin between his thumb and forefinger, all his attention focused on my eyes. "How important is it to you to know what happened, witch?" Cassis asks quietly.

A shiver runs down my spine. "Important."

He cocks a brow. "Are you certain?"

Something about the way Cassis asks the question tightens my stomach. But I raise my chin. "I'm sure."

"All right." Moving faster than I can react, Cassis grabs my shoulders and yanks me around so my back is against him. A scream wells in my throat, but before I can utter the sound, before Ellis and Asher and Reese can react, two sharp knives of pain pierce my neck.

The sting is over almost before it starts.

Releasing me, Cassis spits out a mouthful of my blood and curses. "Opioids and CS3. Whoever drugged our witch is playing for keeps."

AFTER AN HOUR of deliberation and Cassis's calls to his sources confirming that CS3—some designer compulsion serum that's one step short of true brainwashing—has no known antidote, the males conclude that the best thing for me is to be under their direct control for the next week. By which point, the serum should work itself free of my system.

I decide they are overprotective idiots.

"This wasn't a prank," I say, throwing up my hands. "Whoever orchestrated this didn't go through all the trouble to compel me just to put a tack on Asher's chair. Unless we find out what is actually happening, they'll just do it again. And if Victor is involved—which he surely is at some level—the next time he has a go, we may not catch on at all until it's too late."

"What do you want to do?" Ellis asks, cupping my cheek.

I swallow. "Let it play out. Give my secret puppet master an illusion of success while you watch from afar until we know the full intent."

"And what if the full intent is for you to kill yourself?" Asher growls, his tawny eyes almost electric with protective fury. For a moment, he looks more like the wolf than the male. I'm seeing a whole new side of him now that we're mated.

"Then we will interfere before she does so." Ellis traces my cheekbone with his thumb, his confidence in me—and in them—making something glow deep in my core. He gives me a small nod. "I've pushed Devinee to the limit and beyond. She is braver than I wish she was. But that is who she is."

He lowers his forehead to mine, and for a moment, there is nothing more intimate than that touch. That trust.

Then we return to the reality of a much more grudging, skeptical acceptance from the rest of the room. I raise my chin, trying to project the bravery Ellis thinks he sees inside me—and hoping like hell we are doing the right thing.

It's about six in the evening when I get an overwhelming urge to leave my room, leaving an indignant Kitten behind. It's the kind of urgency that overwhelms everything, like a need to use the bathroom that leaves no room for other thought. Slipping quietly up the steps of the dungeon, I step into the cool evening and make my way toward the Academy entrance. Damp grass swishes against my boots, the green a broad stretch of swirling mist and shadows. Moonlight filters down weakly through silver-gray clouds.

With each heartbeat, the certainty that I'm doing something important, something *good,* gathers tighter around me. The possibility of stopping is unthinkable. I close my eyes, trying to shake off the strange sensation, but I can't. I need to get to the front of the Academy. To meet someone.

A sleek black Rolls Royce idles in the circular drive, a tall silhouette standing by a back passenger door.

"Count Victor." Relief floods through me as the vampire opens the car door for me, dark eyes glimmering with a warm welcome.

"It is good to see you, Samantha," he says.

"Likewise." Truth. Now that I see him, my heart slows, my anxiety settling. Now that we're together, I'm one step closer to doing what needs to be done.

Victor gets into the back with me, his sharp face still creased in a pleased smile. "I am glad you decided to come." His eyes widen as he speaks.

Yes. I decided to come. It was my decision.

"Here," Victor holds a flask out to me. "I think you will find this quite agreeable."

"I recommend against that, sir," the driver says, his tight eyes reflecting in the rearview mirror. "The interactions—"

"That will be all, Anton," Victor tells the driver, who quiets immediately. "Go ahead, Samantha. It is a big night today, for us and for the humans we are protecting. This is just something to help you focus."

I take a sip from Victor's flask, the thick sweetness rolling over my tongue. "Cassis liqueur."

Victor nods. "I heard you were a fan."

My pocket vibrates and I pull out my phone, a picture of a rakishly grinning Cassis on the screen.

"Throw it out," Victor tells me, his dark eyes gripping mine again. "You want to keep your friend out of danger."

I do. Rolling down the window, I chuck the phone into the forest. "Cassis wants to find his missing humans," I say, as much to Victor as to myself. I'm not sure why, but it seems important.

I expect Victor to dismiss my words, but he nods instead, leaning toward me. A black curl of hair falls over his pale forehead, softening the effect of his steely but trustworthy gaze. "Yes, he does. The fae have been snatching humans and forcing them through the gateway into Talon for centuries. Your friend Cassis told you as much. You have his word, not just mine. That's why you want to close the gateway to Talon. Because that is the only way to keep everyone safe. Isn't it?"

I blink, tasting the words. The logic. "Yes," I say, meaning it fully. "Yes, it is."

2 8

ASHER

$\mathcal{A}$sher hated the plan to let Samantha be bait. Hated it even more when it became clear that the bastard who'd drugged and compelled her was none other than Victor himself.

Sam was too brave for her own good, and it was harder than it should be for Asher to shove his anxiety for her into the back of his mind. Right now, his job wasn't to worry—it was to make his mate's part count. Sam trusted the horsemen to stop whatever malice Victor intended her for, to be the lifeline that would pull her out.

"They're heading toward the gateway," Cassis said over the speakerphone. "I have a visual on both Victor's Rolls and her reptile."

Asher rubbed his hand absently. Kitten had managed to nip him when he let the dragon out of Sam's room, as if the unjust captivity had somehow been Asher's fault.

"They're going inside," Cassis reported.

"Acknowledged," Reese echoed over the line, Ellis doing the same.

They had taken three cars, Asher riding shotgun with Ellis, who was already giving orders for the staging location they would assemble at. After centuries of walking their own destructive paths, the four of them were back into a single unit. At least for this one evening.

They drove slowly, calmly, through the sleeping outskirts of downtown Talonswood and up the hill toward the towering, modern glass-and-steel structure that housed the ancient gateway deep underneath it. It glowed from within with a faint blue light, all the security lights switched on for the evening.

After pulling to the side of the road just out of sight of the front entrance, they climbed out on silent feet, carefully clicking their doors shut behind them. Asher fell in step behind Ellis, both of their swords strapped down their spines, both clad all in black like the other two. The familiar four-creature formation stoked deep-seated memories. They'd always been stronger together than apart. And with Samantha, they'd be stronger still.

Ellis stopped in the shadows by the broad steel steps leading up to the entrance, his face hard. The gateway building was operated completely by fae; no one even made it past the front lobby without a full security check. "What the hell is Victor doing?" he murmured. "No one is going to allow them past the front door, not unless he subdues security. But that's akin to a declaration of war. A war the vamps have already lost once. What could he want in there so badly that would be worth that?"

Asher frowned, pieces of information from the past months arranging and rearranging themselves in his head. "A war with the fae. Fae who are mostly on the other side of that gateway, not here." His breath froze as the pieces slid into place. "If someone—say a powerful witch—were to close the gateway altogether, the war would be over before it starts."

"It appears you weren't far off when calling the punishment an opportune time for Victor to turn Sam against you," said Reese. "Except the count's target was broader. He was going for the entire fae race."

Asher nodded, other pieces falling into place as well. The closing spell Victor had had the witch learn. The other vamp cadets' sudden friendliness to her. The ease with which Victor had turned the reins of power and discipline over to Asher's hands.

"Once Victor saw Samantha at Dusk, he made it a point to show us both the plane that my missing humans were in," Cassis said, confirming Asher's thoughts. "I believe he wished to ensure I'd discuss snatching with her. Another brick to reinforce the wall. Even with CS3 in the witch's blood, the spell to close the gateway must involve a desire to do so."

"Then let's see if we can't change her mind," said Ellis. His sword was already out, his body half crouched. He'd been watching the dragon, Asher realized. Waiting for Kitten to make entry into the gateway building first so they could ride on the tail of the distraction. "Let's go."

Jogging on light feet, Asher followed Ellis's lead through the door, fully expecting to walk into a chaotic skirmish of vamps and fae.

Silence greeted them instead. Only blue-tinged emergency lights illuminated the large marble entry hall. Two evening security guards sat slumped over at their station.

"They're alive," Cassis said, fingers on the pulse of one of the fae males. "No obvious wounds."

More unconscious guards greeted them as they made their way through the vast, silent building and down one of the elevators to the bottommost floor. The on-duty evening staff all slumped at their posts. On chairs. In the middle of the sterile white corridors. All with no sign of struggle. Ripping off the hem of his shirt, Asher tied it around his mouth and nose, motioning for Ellis to do the same. Not great protection, but better than nothing. An aerosol agent was the most likely culprit—and fit in well with Victor's new preference for drugs —and some must still be in the air, even if Victor had judged it safe to bring Sam inside.

Holding up a hand to bring the group to a stop outside the security office guarding the gateway, Ellis motioned for Asher and Cassis to take point.

Exchanging quick glances for coordination, Asher and Cassis stepped together into the semicircular room, their swords bared. The guard on duty was slumped over too, though someone seemed to have heaved him out of the chair in the midst of all the surveillance monitors. In fact, the dozens of screens were not currently showing live feeds at all, instead displaying loops of historical footage.

Dozens upon dozens of people, some dressed in modern clothing, others wearing sturdy, practical clothing of a different time—showing just how long this had been going on —all bound and forced through the shimmering arched gateway. Sound came from one monitor on which an all-female group under the control of four whip-wielding fae males sobbed and pleaded for release. A couple of the victims flinched away from their captors in a way that made the manner of their abuse all too clear. Asher had known distantly of the practice, but seeing it laid bare made his stomach turn.

Which was exactly the reason Victor had set this up, to shore up Samantha's resolve before pushing her to the next step.

Cassis flipped off the sound, his attention on one particular screen. "Those are *my* humans," he growled under his breath as he settled into the command chair and started flipping more switches to get the cameras back on track and give them a bird's-eye view of the place.

"Ten vamps in the gateway hall," Cassis announced, twisting the camera around until landing on Samantha and Victor, standing at the side of the gateway. "And there she is."

Asher's heart pounded as he leaned in closer, assessing the witch. Unharmed but glassy-eyed. The gateway hall was as somber and imposing as ever. Built in a tall natural cavern, its smooth stone ceiling was nearly perfectly arched, almost like the nave of a mortal cathedral. Magical ever-burning torches had been set into sconces all around the room—set there centuries ago by the very witches who created the gateway. The hall was unfurnished but for one notable exception, a great marble dais right in the center, circular and rimmed with steps so one could approach it from any angle. In the center of the dais, a simple stone arch, filled with what looked like shimmering silver air.

"Weapons?" Ellis asked.

Taking up the secondary controls, Asher forced himself to tear his gaze away from Sam to review the enemy force. "Not overt ones. They seem to be wearing lab coats, actually."

Smart. A gathering of vampire warriors on Talonswood would have attracted attention, but the researchers lived here for decades at a time. Victor was leading a surgical strike. A bloodless revolution indeed.

"He's having her start drawing the rune." Asher swung off his chair, only his years of training keeping him from rushing blindly into the chamber. "We don't have more time."

Ellis nodded, a deadly calm on his face. "Let's move."

Unlike Victor's approach, there was nothing civilized about the savage way Ellis slit two researchers' throats before the horsemen were fully inside the gateway chamber, or the way Cassis snapped another neck without so much as a pause.

Trusting the others to keep the interference at bay, Asher sheathed his sword and stepped forward from the shadows at the edge of the hall, the phantom wind of the place cool against his skin.

The circular dais shimmered with the silver reflection from the portal, the light tinting Samantha's pale skin. She was already crouched by the base of the stone arch, her finger dipped into a chalice Victor held beside her. The count clearly knew they were there, but he kept his gaze trained on the witch, curving protectively over her like he cared for her welfare. He carried no weapons—nothing to scare off Sam and break the compulsion—but a vampire didn't need one.

Intuitively, Asher knew that Victor would never kill her— she was too useful—but he could hurt her. Badly. And the vamp knew that was leverage enough.

Circling above, Kitten flapped his wings in agitation, alternately crying his warning and puffing streams of fire that flashed in the dim room.

"Samantha!" Asher called, pitching his voice over the cavern. He was twenty feet away. Too far to make a leap for her.

The witch looked up. Her hazel gaze was glassy, sweat streaking down the sides of her face despite the room's chill. Victor had drugged her again.

"Asher." Sam blinked at him. "What are you doing here?"

Asher's heart pounded. He wished he could fight this with blade and blood, but he couldn't. Not with Victor so much closer to his mate than he was.

"Samantha," he said again, holding his empty hands up toward her. "Listen to me. Victor drugged you. Closing the gateway is what he wants, not you."

Victor settled his free hand on the witch's shoulder, long pale fingers curling solicitously over her flesh. "Commander

Asher just wants power for himself, Samantha. He's a tyrant. Like so many you grew up with. Don't take my word for it, take your own. What did he do when he had power? How did he treat you? How did he treat others?"

Asher flinched.

Samantha hesitated. Blinked. Something red dripped from her hand. Blood.

"Think of the slaves, Samantha," Victor continued in his calm, hypnotic voice. "This is the only way to ensure the fae can never take them again."

"No, it isn't." Asher took another step forward. "We will find the criminal responsible. But if you close the gateway, there will be no balance to the vampires' rule. To Victor's rule. You think he'll treat the humans well when there's no one for him to answer to?"

"I only want peace, Samantha," Victor said, his dark eyes flashing with quickly suppressed fury. "I've never lied to you. But the fae have. Who set you up to be sent to Talonswood Reform? Who tried to keep you from learning your magic? Who attacked the Academy?" The vampire knelt down beside Samantha, placing the chalice before her on the marble. "Look around the room now. At the blood that's been spilled. I've kept things peaceful. They have not." He turned Sam toward him, his pupils widening. "Finish drawing the rune. Now."

Samantha dipped her finger in the chalice.

"Devinee, don't." Stepping up beside Asher, Ellis added his voice. "Look at me, Sam. Remember who I am. Who we are. I am your mate."

Sam flinched. Hesitated.

"I am your mate, Samantha," Reese's British accent filled the hall, the vampire standing shoulder to shoulder with Ellis.

"Trust me." He held his hand out to her. "Join us. We need each other."

"I am your mate," Asher said, ripping his shirtsleeve open to show his mark. "Fight Victor's compulsion. You can do it."

Sam shook herself violently, her eyes clearing for a moment. Rose. Slowly. Carefully.

Asher's heart pounded against his chest, his breath still. He wanted to rush forward and grab his mate, but Victor was still too close to her to risk it. For Asher to risk it—but perhaps not for Cassis. In the side of his vision, Asher saw the vamp flowing through the flickering shadows, taking advantage of the distraction to get himself into position for backup intervention.

"Samantha," Victor's voice took on a note of warning, his gaze cutting to a vamp on the right side of the chamber when Samantha failed to respond. "Anton, what's happening?"

"I warned you the serum was experimental, sir." The silver-haired vampire in a white lab coat raised his arms. "Desire is delicate. It can't be bottled and stressed."

Cassis was almost in position. Just a few more seconds of distraction. Asher took another small step toward the dais. "Remember what you said you wanted—"

"Enough of this. Bring him!" Victor bared his teeth, his face transforming from hypnotic calm to deadly determination. "I'd watch your words, Commander Asher. What happens next is entirely up to you."

Before Asher could respond, a small door in the side of the cavern opened, and Raulle the cook manhandled Jake into the chamber. Blood drained from Asher's face as the vamp shoved the small whimpering boy onto the dais, the vest of explosives strapped to him flashing in many colorful rows, the wires extending down the boy's arms and legs.

Sam stood frozen, her confused eyes wide in question.

"What happens next is simple," Victor instructed, reclaiming his composure while Asher's whole body vibrated with tension. "First, the idiot who thinks I don't see him moving toward the dais is going to stop, drop his weapon to the floor, and step forward. Otherwise, I press the button that starts the charge." He held up a remote.

It was hard to speak, Asher's heart pounded so hard. He stared at his son, at that striped polo he still wore from yesterday, at the dark shadows under his big golden-brown eyes. "You don't want to kill your only hostage, Victor," he said. "Let's talk about this."

"Kill?" Victor's brows rose. "What kind of barbarian do you think I am to kill a child? The explosives will simply remove a limb at a time. Now then, Cassis—step forward, or I will start with the right hand."

Hot acid rose up Asher's throat, his body so still, it ached.

At the side of the chamber, Cassis stepped forward as instructed, dropping his sword on the floor.

"Victor…" Sam's voice sounded glazed and sleepy. "This isn't right. We don't want violence."

"You are exactly right," Victor reassured the girl, his dark eyes widening again as he looked her way. "See? I've made an attacker drop his sword. We need to stop bloodshed, you and I. The sooner you can draw the rune, the sooner everyone goes home. Safe." He turned to Asher. "I know you agree, Commander. In fact, why don't you explain to Samantha just how much she *wants* to close the gateway. Do that, and no one needs to get hurt. Fail and, well…" He lifted the remote, and a light on Jack's vest shifted.

"Father!" Jake called, tears streaming down his face. "Help me. Please. I don't want to die."

"Of course you don't," said Victor. "Hang tight, Jake, and

Samantha will help you. She'll make sure you are safe. You and many others."

"Samantha, please." Jake turned his eyes on the witch. "Don't let him hurt me."

"I won't," Samantha whispered, her words swimming as if she were drunk. "You're going to be okay, Jake. I promise." Picking up the chalice of blood she'd been using for the rune, Sam dipped her hand in it again, drawing a fresh line over the drying lines of the rune that had been interrupted.

"I want to protect humans," she said, her gaze flickering up, touching Cassis's. Asher's. "Think of your missing humans."

Asher had only a heartbeat to register the choice of words, the crystal-clear hazel eyes that met his, before the phantom wind in the room picked up power.

Victor twisted toward the commotion.

And that moment was all it took for Sam to leap forward, grab Jake, and throw the pair of them through the shimmering gateway to Talon.

To Cassis's missing humans.

To where the explosive triggers of the modern world were as useless as cell phones.

Finish the adventure - and enjoy crossover guest stars from the POWER OF FIVE series - is LAST CHANCE WORLD, IMMORTALS OF TALONSWOOD Book 4.

Young Adult Fantasy Novels

TIDES

FIRST COMMAND (Audiobook available)

AIR AND ASH (Audiobook available)

WAR AND WIND (Audiobook available)

SEA AND SAND (Audiobook available)

SCOUT

TRACING SHADOWS (Audiobook available)

UNRAVELING DARKNESS (Audiobook available)

TILDOR

THE CADET OF TILDOR

SIGN UP FOR NEW RELEASE NOTIFICATIONS at https://links.alexlidell.com/News

ABOUT THE AUTHOR

Alex Lidell is an Amazon KU All Star Top 50 Author Awards winner (July, 2018). Her debut novel, THE CADET OF TILDOR (Penguin, 2013) was an Amazon Breakout Novel Awards finalist. Her Reverse Harem romances, POWER OF FIVE and MISTAKE OF MAGIC, both received Amazon KU Top 100 awards for individual titles.

Alex is an avid horseback rider, a (bad) hockey player, and an ice-cream addict. Born in Russia, Alex learned English in elementary school, where a thoughtful librarian placed a copy of Tamora Pierce's ALANNA in Alex's hands. In addition to becoming the first English book Alex read for fun, ALANNA started Alex's life long love for fantasy books. Alex lives in Washington, DC.

Join Alex's newsletter for news, special offers and sneak peeks: https://links.alexlidell.com/News

Find out more on Alex's website: www.alexlidell.com

SIGN UP FOR NEWS AND RELEASE NOTIFICATIONS

Connect with Alex!
www.alexlidell.com
alex@alexlidell.com